MOUNTAIN TOUGH

STORIES OF MOUNTAIN MYSTERY AND SURVIVAL

ROBIN BRANDE

Mountain Tough
Stories of Mountain Mystery and Survival
By Robin Brande

Published by Ryer Publishing
www.ryerpublishing.com
Copyright 2022, 2026 by Robin Brande
www.robinbrande.com
Art by HayDmitriy and DonyaNedomam/Depositphotos
Digiartz Studio/Canva
Ebook ISBN: 978-1-952383-08-3
Paperback ISBN: 978-1-952383-30-4

"On Red Mountain" was first published in *Pulphouse Magazine #12*, 2021.

"Taken at Rustler Pass" was first published in *Pulphouse Magazine #40*, 2025.

ALSO BY ROBIN BRANDE

<u>Winnie Parsons Mysteries</u>

A Mind for Mysteries (Collection)

The Genius Track

A Man of Appetites

A Drop of Sweat

The Long Gray Hook

The Slip of a Rib

The Cabin Ghost

The Secret Juror

The Truth Chamber

<u>Dove Season Universe</u>

Dove Season

Finder

Seeker

Believer

Maker

Explorer

<u>Young Adult</u>

Evolution, Me & Other Freaks of Nature

Fat Cat

Doggirl

Replay

Into the Parallel

Caught in the Parallel

Seize the Parallel

Beyond the Parallel

Book of Earth

Book of Water

<u>Romance</u>

Love Proof

Freefall

Heart of Ice

Fire and Ice

<u>Self-Help</u>

What If You're Doing It Right?

What If You're Doing It Right? For Teens

<u>Collections</u>

The Love of a Good Dog

Mountain Tough

The Miraculous Unknown

Life with the Afterlife

Heart of the Future

MOUNTAIN TOUGH

CONTENTS

ON RED MOUNTAIN

Lightning death. He's dead. He died. That really happened.

Rafe's body was starting to go cold. Aubrey's was, too. Rain and hail had been lashing down on her for the past half hour, but all she could think about was doing CPR and rescue breathing because even if lightning stopped a heart it didn't mean the person was dead.

She had eight years training and experience as a Wilderness First Responder. She knew things. She knew she might get his heart going again, but the respiratory system could still be down. She might have to do rescue breathing for an hour. He might still live. It was up to her.

But now she was starting to shake. She hadn't done

the rest of it right. It's like a flight, her instructor had said. Oxygen masks drop, and you have to put yours on first. You have to make sure you save yourself before you can save anyone else.

Aubrey was shaking and she knew it was hypothermia. She hadn't dug out her rain coat and rain pants when Rafe went down, she had gotten right to it, cold rain beating against her face and body, one, two, three, pumping his chest, chanting the song that the WFRs all knew to get the rhythm right, the one from *Saturday Night Fever* about stayin' alive.

She checked the pulse again, but he was dead. She had to understand that. Her brain felt slow and weak. *I'm going to die*, it told her, *I'm going to die of hypothermia, stop, save yourself, you're shivering. THIS IS IMPORTANT.*

Aubrey dragged her attention away from her husband's face. He was cold and dead. They were alone on the high treeless ridge of Red Mountain. No one was around. They hadn't seen any other backpackers for days. It was why they came here. Solitude was a feature, not a flaw.

Until now. *Think, think.* She had to take steps. There were things to do now that his heart had never restarted and the breathing never came. Things to do. *Put on your rain gear. You're soaked through. You'll die up here.*

Where was she? It had finally come to this. All these years of promising herself she'd finally pay attention to wilderness navigation, but that was Rafe's job. It was boring, she told him, so she had been the one to go get medical training.

Now she was four days from the trailhead. Go forward? Go back? Which was faster?

What should she do with Rafe's body?

Aubrey panted in the cold wet air. Her heart was out of control, racing ahead, trying to keep her warm and alive.

I don't know where I am. That was Rafe's job.

Not anymore.

2

At the grocery store. Aubrey is six.

Her mother is drunk. It isn't even noon yet.

But the autumn is hard for Aubrey's mother. She will turn another year older in October which means another year further away from being young and beautiful. She consoles herself about it for months.

Aubrey knows the shopping list by heart. Skim milk, Special K because her mother is always on a diet and some skinny celebrity said she always eats Special K, fiber bars, and two apples.

Aubrey collects those things while her mother goes to the liquor aisle.

They meet up at the register.

The cashier, a pasty-faced woman who looks like

the lunch lady at school and whose name tag says Constance, is new.

"Whoo-hoo! Breakfast of champions!" she says cheerfully as she rings up the cereal and five bottles of vodka.

That vodka will be gone even before the cereal is.

Aubrey looks up at her mother. She wonders what she'll do.

What she'll do is look bleary-eyed at Constance and say, "Mind your own damn business, whore."

The air seems to stand still for a moment. Aubrey looks at the cashier. Her pasty face has gone even whiter. Aubrey can smell perspiration sprout from the woman's armpits.

Aubrey's mother is staring back at her, a hateful, challenging look on her face.

"Where you go to school, honey?" Constance the Cashier asks Aubrey in a voice that still sounds cheerful, but also shaky.

Aubrey looks at her mother. She isn't sure whether she should answer.

"Did I not say it's none of your damn business?" Aubrey's mother repeats in a much louder voice this time. "*Whore?*"

The manager, Mr. Davies, is rushing over. This isn't the first time.

"Now, now..." he says, but to Constance the Cashier, not the drunk customer.

Aubrey's mother rounds on him. "How much do we spend here, Frank?"

He's nodding like his head is a bobble toy. "Yes, yes, Mrs. Fry. Of course." He starts bagging the groceries himself, even though a teenage bag boy has been standing there gaping the whole time. "Move over, Kyle," Mr. Davies murmurs, and the neatly-dressed bag boy does.

Aubrey notices his shoes. Very white sneakers. So white he must scrub them every night.

The store makes him wear a tie. All the bag boys do. The only bag girl Aubrey has ever seen wears a knit shirt with a collar and always has her hair up in a neat ponytail.

Aubrey would rather notice all of this than watch her mother buy five more bottles of vodka every two days.

"Come on, we're going to the store."

Every other day.

Aubrey's mother always waits until Aubrey is home from school or is hanging around the house on a weekend. Like there's some insurance in bringing her six-year-old with her. Maybe she thinks nobody will say anything in front of her daughter.

Aubrey always hopes that, too. Constance the Cashier might have learned her lesson.

Aubrey had to learn her lesson, too. She used to try

to get out of going to the store, but the penalties were always too high.

"Oh, I guess you don't want to take lunch this week."

"Oh, I guess Rally doesn't need dog food this week."

"Guess your dad won't have his burgers. I'll tell him you couldn't be bothered."

Now Aubrey tags along without ever complaining and does all the other grocery shopping while her mother is busy.

On the drive home, Aubrey's mother smokes a Virginia Slims and blows her smoke out the open window. Out of the corner of her eye Aubrey can see the smirk on her face for having gotten Constance in trouble.

Aubrey watches the road.

Two months ago, when it was still summer and her mother only needed four bottles of vodka every two days, on the way back from the store she misjudged the curb and drove right through a stop sign and into a tree.

Eight months ago, in the car they had before this one, she didn't see the stoplight and kept on going and a yellow Buick LeSabre hit them broadside. It was on Aubrey's side, just behind her seat. Aubrey's mother got a ticket that she was furious about.

But they all know Oscar Fry's wife likes her drink. Oscar Fry brings a lot of business to the town. Oscar Fry will smooth things over. It's fine.

Aubrey watches the road and that's how she knows her mother has made a wrong turn.

"No, back there," she says quietly. "Mom, it's left on Turner."

Aubrey's mother leans forward and squints through the windshield like that will give her any information.

"Oh," is all she says.

Then she makes a U-turn right on the spot.

The driver of the white Ford pickup behind them isn't expecting it. Why should he. He slams on his brakes and honks and Aubrey looks back and can see his wide, alarmed eyes.

The Ford pickup just barely misses them.

Aubrey closes her eyes and mouths to whoever might be listening, *thank you thank you thank you.*

As Turner Street comes closer, Aubrey points to it. Politely.

"There, Mom."

Her mother nods in her own bobble-headed way. She makes the turn.

They get home safely.

Aubrey has learned every street within ten miles of their house.

She knows where her mother can turn whenever she gets lost along the route.

She is her drunk mother's co-pilot. Her navigator. Her shopping assistant. Her buffer.

She has had to grab the steering wheel more times

than she can remember to try to keep the car going straight.

She can't reach the brakes, though, and her mother has run over two cats and one dog and kept on driving.

Aubrey prays it won't ever be a person.

3

On the summit of Red Mountain.

Go back.

Backward is a known quantity. Forward is not.

Backward was four days up, but Aubrey thought she could probably do it in three.

Take what?

She had put her rain gear on finally, for all the good it would do. Every inch of clothing underneath it was soaked.

But it did provide some windbreak, so that was something at least.

But Aubrey was still shivering. Rafe was still dead.

His skin was growing chalkier by the minutes.

She had seen him deathly ill before, with dark circles under his eyes standing out against the pale skin of his normally tanned and rugged face, and she could almost believe it now, that he was just sick, if she didn't know the truth.

Dragging his body back with her wasn't an option.

Pitching the tent right here and dragging him into it wasn't either.

And she needed the tent for herself. For tonight and at least one more, maybe two more nights.

The rain and wind were still beating on her. Whatever she was going to do, she had to do it quickly.

Quickly and mechanically and mindlessly. Otherwise she might start to fall apart.

She got the pack off his stiffening arms. Dug in there for his sleeping bag so neatly compressed in its yellow waterproof sack.

Opened the sack, pulled out the sleeping bag. Unzipped it all the way.

It was a mummy bag with a zipper down the left side. Aubrey had a matching mummy bag with the zipper on the right. That way they could zip them together at night in a bag for two and cuddle up together.

The zippers only went down three-quarters of the way, ending at the footwell, about mid-shin. Aubrey pulled the bottom of the sleeping bag over Rafe's boots. Then she had to shimmy the rest of his body inside.

It took her longer than she expected. His body

didn't cooperate. Dead weight. But finally she managed to pull the entire bag around him and zip him up. Then she tugged the mummy hood over the back of his head and cinched it tight.

The only thing exposed now was his lifeless, handsome face. Aubrey dug out his extra polypro long john top and laid it over his face and tucked it into the hood all around.

Rain quickly soaked all of it. Down bags never did well once they got wet. But Rafe didn't need to stay warm. He just needed some protection from scavenging birds and animals. However long such a scanty covering might last.

Aubrey could see the outline of his face beneath the thin cloth.

She leaned forward and kissed his lips. They weren't so cold through the fabric.

Then with a sharp pain in her chest she took off half hiking, half running along the trail.

A bright white burst of lightning snapped at her overhead. The crash of thunder followed too quickly.

It was still right over her. She had been lucky so far. Lightning could have struck her too, any minute.

She was tempting fate, tempting death.

Aubrey abandoned her husband and ran for her life.

4

———————————

"Hey, doll."

"Handsome."

Aubrey's mother is sitting in her floral upholstered chair, very straight-backed, smoking a Slims and drinking vodka from a tumbler.

Aubrey's father gives his wife a full-lipped kiss on the lips. He licks his own lips and murmurs, "Mmmm."

Aubrey is sitting on the rose-colored carpeting playing with Safari Barbie and Barbie's little sister Safari Stacie. They are both dressed impractically in very short shorts, pink of course, and hiking boots that look they might sprain their ankles.

But Aubrey doesn't know that. She loves the clothes.

Rally the Golden Retriever stands in for all the

jungle animals: lions, tigers, monkeys, whatever Barbie and Stacie might see through their bright pink binoculars.

"Hey, kiddo." Aubrey's father reaches down and tousles her hair.

Aubrey looks up at him, adoring. She pops to her feet.

She races to the kitchen to get there before he does. She knows exactly what he likes. Wild Turkey 101, up. That means with no ice. She pours him a tumbler of his own and hands it to him.

"Thank you, waitress," he says.

She loves that he's willing to pretend.

Then he tousles her hair one more time and goes back into the living room to sit in his chair.

He turns on the TV to watch the news.

That's Aubrey's signal to gather up her Barbies and go play somewhere else.

But she dawdles a little, waiting to hear what her mother will say about the car.

After the dramatic U-turn and the almost collision with the Ford pickup, Aubrey must not have said enough silent thank yous.

Because a block later, on Adams Street, her mother sideswiped somebody's brick mailbox. The mailbox itself was up on top of the brick pillar, and undamaged. But the bricks beneath it exploded apart.

When they got home, Aubrey's mother examined

the side of the car and muttered, "Shit." The bricks were painted white. They left a deep dent and white streaks of paint on the right front side of the black Mercedes.

Aubrey's mother opened the trunk and took out her two bags of bottles. She left it open so Aubrey could bring in the rest of the groceries.

But Aubrey has stretched out picking up her Barbies as long as she can, and her father still hasn't said anything about the car.

Maybe he didn't notice on his way in.

Some part of Aubrey wishes her mother would get in trouble, just one time.

5

The storm continued charging at Aubrey the entire length of the ridge.

With each crash of thunder her heart rate doubled. Doubled again.

Next time. That's going to be the one. I'm not going to make it. It's going to kill me.

Her wet clothing underneath the rain gear clung against her skin. But the running had given her some warmth at last.

Running and constant fear.

There was a smell in the air that she was used to thinking of as ozone, but now she thought it might be more like liquid fire. Like lighter fluid just as it met with a flame. That sort of chemical, sickly scent.

What will Rafe smell like?

Aubrey thought she knew. She had been out on a two-day call with Search and Rescue once, right after she got her certification. The rescue became a body recovery.

The missing hiker had fallen down a scree field and broken his neck and back. They doubted he survived the fall, but if he did, it would have been for only a short while, and that short while would have been hell.

So he might have been dead anywhere up to two days.

One of the rescuers on the team sniffed the air and said, "Cheesy."

To Aubrey it smelled more like dirty socks and unwashed body. Like the dorm room of a guy she dated briefly in college. Dirty laundry everywhere.

They all put on their face masks. That was protocol. But it barely cut the smell.

Since it was a recovery now, the burly men in the group were the ones to rope down to the body and then rope it back up. Aubrey was assigned communication. She had to hike until she found a reasonably flat and safe landing area for the helicopter. She waited there to call it in and coordinate. By the time she came in contact with the body again, the helicopter team had a body bag to seal it up in.

Aubrey would have to find a landing site for them to get Rafe.

But first she had to get down from this ridge, alive.

6

Aubrey is fourteen.

It is only the second week of her freshman year at Klondike High.

One of the older kids comes into her government class and hands the teacher a note. It's on peach-colored paper, which means it came from the office.

Mrs. Denreid reads it and looks up. "Aubrey Fry?"

Aubrey gets a cold, sick feeling in her heart.

She has no premonition. Nothing supernatural. Just the constant daily dread of wondering what will happen next.

Through the glass door of the office she can see her neighbor, a nice grandmotherly woman named Mrs. Thompson.

Mrs. Thompson turns around and sees her. She lifts a wad of tissues to her nose.

It's like a dream now, slow motion, as Aubrey pushes through the glass door and walks in a stately pace into Mrs. Thompson's outstretched arms.

Aubrey lets the neighbor woman fold her inside her warm, protective bulk.

She can feel Mrs. Thompson shaking with suppressed tears as she tries to get the words out.

"Your father—"

Aubrey wails. She doesn't have to hear anything else.

She wishes the second word was *mother*.

Now Aubrey will have to take care of everything herself.

7

It took over an hour for Aubrey to make treeline. She felt safe again, under the trees.

If lightning struck here, it would take one of the spruce or fir. Aubrey was tiny and inconspicuous now in comparison to the overall canopy above her.

Finally, she could rest.

Although not for very long.

She needed to find a landing spot. Needed to mark it for the helicopter pilot.

There was protocol. A list. Tasks to check off.

But she shucked off her pack and sat on the dirt underneath the trees and gave her mind over to what had really happened.

She was a widow now, just like her mother.

Nothing like my mother.

She had spent her husband's last living night lying in his arms, both of them so properly tired out from the long day's backpacking they were probably awake together a total of ten minutes.

She kissed him. She remembered that. Told him she loved him. She always said that before they went to sleep.

He said the same. She turned her back to him and snuggled into the curve of his body and his arms.

Earlier in the day they talked about getting another dog. Their old one had died over the winter.

"I want a girl this time," Aubrey told him. "Too much man energy in the house."

"One each," Rafe said. "Brother and sister."

It reminded Aubrey of a story she read when she was a little girl. About a brother and sister dog who fought against a mountain lion to save the boy who raised them.

The dogs didn't survive. Aubrey read those pages of the book and cried so hard she made noises that woke up her parents.

How the school librarian could recommend that book to a third-grade girl, Aubrey still didn't under-stand. It should come with a warning: *This will break your heart. Read at your own risk.*

But she still remembered those dogs' names. She told Rafe that's what they'd call their own.

Maybe it was a bad omen, naming dogs after dogs who had died.

Or maybe it was just more proof that at any time something could come along to break your heart.

She allowed herself only a half hour's rest. She needed to keep moving. She needed to find help. She had to hurry back the way they came—

That's when she realized.

She forgot the map.

Not only the map, but half of all the gear she would need.

It was back in Rafe's pack, lying beside his body on the ridge.

The map. The stove. The tent.

Aubrey carried the tent poles, for all the good they would do. And she carried all the food, but now had no way to cook it.

She had no matches. Those were in the emergency kit at the bottom of Rafe's pack, along with the compass and the signaling mirror.

Even though Aubrey already knew all the contents of her own pack, now she frantically pulled out every item to make sure.

Her sleeping bag with the compatible zipper so she could snuggle up to Rafe. A set of dry clothes. Fleece hat and gloves.

A waterproof sack to hold three more days of

meals. Breakfasts of instant coffee, packets of oatmeal, and sliced peaches she dehydrated herself.

Rafe's favorite dinners Aubrey cooked and also dehydrated herself: shepherd's pie with peas and mashed potatoes; angel hair pasta with a garlicky spaghetti sauce; ramen noodles mixed with shredded cabbage, spices, and cashews.

But Rafe carried the lunch foods. The crackers and tubes full of peanut butter. The food Aubrey could have eaten without a stove.

It was all so stupid. No foresight at all. Either in the packing or before she started running off the ridge.

When she took out Rafe's sleeping bag to cover him, she should have noticed all the other things she would need.

But she didn't. That was real. There was no point in pretending. She had to figure out what to do about it.

She checked her water supply. Half a bag left.

The water filter was in Rafe's pack, too.

She could still drink water from any of the streams, it just meant that she might get a parasite because of it.

No stove, no tent, no matches. No map, no compass, no filter.

Aubrey looked up at the dark sky she hid from beneath the trees.

She had to go back. There was nothing for it.

And there was no point in waiting. She had to go now.

8

Aubrey is nineteen.

Her sophomore year in college.

An hour and a half away from home, if she drives over the speed limit.

But she drives home slowly this Thursday in October because her mother is already dead.

Not a peach-colored note from the office this time. Not the kindly neighbor woman waiting to hug her.

A call from a police officer assigned to the case.

"I'm afraid your mother was considerably over the limit."

For a moment Aubrey thinks he means the speed limit. That doesn't surprise her at all.

But it's the alcohol limit. As if that has ever meant

anything to Aubrey's mother. Her blood has been saturated with it for at least the last nineteen years.

Aubrey drives sixty even though the speed limit is sixty-five. She's in no hurry to deal with the mess.

Her mother's latest Mercedes rolled down an embankment. It flipped over and landed on the roof.

"We tried to get her out," the police officer says.

"That's okay," Aubrey mumbles before she hangs up.

At the morgue she has the option of viewing her mother's face on a computer screen.

But it won't seem real that way, so she has them show her the whole thing. The mangled face. The caved-in skull. Her mother's emaciated alcoholic body she was always so proud to keep slim.

She would have died, one way or another. Lung cancer. Liver disease. Heart attack.

Car crash.

Aubrey is only thankful—*so thankful*—her mother didn't kill anyone else in the process.

There had been three more cats she ran over and another dog, but still not a person. Aubrey clings to that.

She stares down at her mother's ruined face.

After a while the morgue attendant has the kindness to pull the white sheet back up over it.

"Must be hard," the attendant says. She looks about

thirty, Native American, with sturdy hands and a compassionate face.

Aubrey looks up then. She has been staring at the sheet. She meets the woman's warm brown eyes.

"I don't think I'm sorry," Aubrey says, surprised by herself. Surprised to know that it's true.

"My mom had the same problem," the attendant says. "Wasn't a day when she wasn't drunk. I'm probably not supposed to say that, but…" She shrugs.

Aubrey nods. The sisterhood of drunk mothers.

"You alone now?" the woman asks.

Aubrey nods.

The attendant reaches over and squeezes Aubrey's hand. She's probably not supposed to do that, either.

Aubrey squeezes back and they share a brief smile, then Aubrey departs the cold and stark dead room.

9

B y late afternoon the storm had shifted enough to the east that Aubrey felt like she was stalking it all the way back to the ridge on top of Red Mountain.

There were no good landing sites for a helicopter anywhere along the way.

All of the terrain was too steep and rugged.

But Aubrey scaled it with a single-minded focus. She climbed it in half the time it took her when she and Rafe first scaled several hours ago.

"You're a real mountain woman," Rafe liked to tell her. He knew how proud it made her feel.

She was a city girl. She grew up on paved streets and in a fancy house. Her mother believed in two showers a day. When she wasn't passed out.

But the first time Rafe took Aubrey out camping, she was surprised by how much she loved the dirt.

She was twenty then, a junior in college. Rafe was in her abnormal psychology class. He was an action adventure hero come to life.

Tall, tan, athletic. Always dressed in outdoorsy clothes, like he was about to jump into his Jeep and take off for the hills.

Dark brown hair that looked tousled from the wind, even when there wasn't any wind.

Clever questions for the professor. A clever smile for Aubrey on their first day of class.

He sat beside her. She glanced over at him in surprise. She had noticed him when he came in, but she didn't think he could have possibly noticed her.

There were a lot of empty chairs. He could have sat anywhere else.

"Which one are you?" he asked, nudging his chin toward the front of the lecture hall at the name of the class written on the white board.

Aubrey thought about it for a moment. She knew it was a test, and she wanted to get this right.

"Psych," she said.

"Good," he said with that handsome smile of his. "If you said abnormal, I'd have to move on."

One of her professors during her first year said most psych majors were trying to heal some trauma about either their families or themselves.

She told that to Rafe on their first date. He laughed and pointed to his chest and said, "Dead brother. Guess it's true."

He took her to bed, he took her outdoors, he took her into a life she never could have imagined.

They got married in their senior year. Neither of them saw any reason to wait.

They were both twenty-nine now. Rafe would be twenty-nine forever.

Aubrey might be the same, unless she could figure this all out.

She could see the bright blue mummy bag now, there on the thin trail at the top of the ridge.

Aubrey's heart pounded. She was coming back. She hadn't abandoned him after all.

The decision came to her quickly. A second chance she needed to take.

When she reached the sleeping bag and his pack, she knelt down and instantly got to work. She took from Rafe's backpack everything she needed.

She left his clothes, but brought everything else. Even his headlamp and the loose-leaf notebook pages he used as a journal.

She would read them tonight. When she and Rafe were safe somewhere else. Off of this damn ridge. Somewhere she could protect him.

She repacked her backpack. Not everything fit. She took it all out and tried again.

It would be heavy, much heavier than she normally carried, but she could do it. She had no choice.

But she did have a choice about Rafe.

Whether to bring him or leave him behind.

She stared down at his covered face. At the navy blue polypro shirt tucked into the bright blue hood of the mummy bag.

She would try it without wearing the backpack first. Just to see if she could do it.

She crouched down and grasped the mummy bag at the shoulders. Then she began dragging Rafe's body backwards.

She had to look back at the trail every other step to make sure she wouldn't lose her footing.

The bottom of the sleeping bag snagged on the rocks. She heard part of it rip. The whole bag was too delicate.

The trail was rocky. It wasn't smooth dirt like inside a forest. And Rafe was heavy.

This wasn't going to work.

Aubrey stopped dragging him and looked behind her. The trail only got rougher from here.

She had moved him maybe ten or fifteen feet.

It had taken her too long to do it.

The muscles of her arms were burning from the effort. Her heart and lungs had to work too hard.

Aubrey heard a rumble off in the distance. She

looked behind her. A new storm was coming. She could see the telltale streaks of gray coming down from a dark bank of clouds. There was rain back there, coming here.

And with it, more thunder and lightning.

Aubrey's pulse quickened.

It was all about to happen again.

Only this time she had a pack that felt twice as heavy. And before long she would lose daylight. She had to get down.

But her husband's body lay at her feet.

She had to face it. She couldn't bring him.

Don't be a second victim.

It was something her Wilderness First Responder instructor drilled into all of their heads.

If the scene wasn't safe enough to go in and rescue someone, you had to be smart and not just go running in, and end up hurt or killed yourself.

"If it's nighttime," the instructor said. "If it's a blizzard. If there's a rockfall. If there's a rattlesnake or crocodile guarding the body—" That got a laugh, but he was serious. "—you need to wait for conditions to improve. Or go get more help. But for godssake, don't make my work twice as hard because now I have to save you too."

Aubrey looked up at the sky again. At the dark heavy clouds storming toward her.

She got what she came for. She still had to leave him. She went back for her pack, now full of what she needed.

And once again, she told Rafe goodbye.

10

Aubrey is twenty-one.

She is a day away from being a bride.

They are in Pinedale, Wyoming where they just finished backpacking in the Wind River range. Rafe proposed to her on a mountain top. Aubrey said yes before he even finished the question.

They pay thirty dollars for a marriage license in Pinedale. The application asks for the bride's mother's maiden name.

Aubrey hasn't thought of her mother for what feels like a long time. Yet here she is again.

If she were alive, she would be drunk at the wedding. Drunk at the reception. Drunk the next morning.

Aubrey doesn't drink at all herself. Rafe has a beer here and there, but not much more.

As she stands next to Rafe in front of the officiant they've hired, a nice older lady who also works at the front desk of the Best Western where they're staying, Aubrey can't help but feel a momentary pang that her father isn't still alive to walk her down an aisle.

But then the short ceremony is over and she is Rafe's wife for life.

The woman from the Best Western takes a picture right then, just as Aubrey and Rafe finish their kiss and stand looking at each other, smiling.

Every time Aubrey looks at the picture she can still see it: the absolute joy she didn't think she'd ever feel.

She can see it on Rafe's face in the picture, too. The boy who lost his twin brother in a car crash when they were sixteen. But happy now. Happy again.

They spend one more night in the Best Western. But then they have to get back home to their summer jobs.

"Forty kids and twelve dogs," Rafe proposes.

"Let's start with one," Aubrey says. "Then we'll see."

They stop at the Pinedale animal shelter on their way out of town.

There's a dog who looks like he's been waiting just for them.

It was nearly dark before Aubrey reached the safety of the forest again. The last few miles she hiked in rain.

Her clothes were almost dry inside her rain gear.

She had to stop thinking of how cold and wet Rafe must be.

He's dead. He doesn't care. He can't feel it.

But it still felt so unreal.

She wondered if she should have kept trying.

He wasn't like her mother, lying mangled in the morgue. He still had so much life in his handsome face.

If she had kept doing CPR longer. Maybe his respiration would have come back.

She gave up too soon.

But you were hypothermic.

And honey, I was dead.

She could hear him, his reasonable voice in her ear, but it was just her imagination trying to soothe her.

If she had taken just a minute to put on her rain gear, she could have kept doing rescue breathing until he came back.

But she failed. She panicked. She ignored all the rules. What was the point of going through all that training as a WFR, just to forget all of it when she needed it most?

The grief was starting to bubble up in her throat.

She had to keep it down. There was still too much to do.

The rain was still pounding while she erected the tent. It was so much easier to do with two people. But she managed to pitch it without getting it too wet inside. She set her pack inside the vestibule and climbed in.

She unpacked everything she needed for her nest: the single mummy bag, her clothing, her headlamp.

She took out the plastic bag Rafe used to hold the loose leaf pages of his journal and his pen so none of them would get wet.

She attached the mini propane bottle to the back-packing stove and set them just outside the vestibule. She stuck a small pot on top and poured in what was left of her water. She would have to go filter some more from the nearest stream later.

Rafe always liked her spaghetti dinner best. She would only need to cook half.

While the meal was rehydrating and boiling, Aubrey changed into dry long johns and a dry fleece top.

When the food was ready she ate directly out of the pot. No need to split into two bowls anymore.

She barely tasted it.

She ate to keep warm.

The rain showed no signs of leaving. She dressed in her rain gear again and took the pot and her water bag down to the stream.

She did a quick rinse of the pot and threw the debris into a nearby bush. The rain would drown it before any animals came sniffing.

She used the filter to pump a fresh bag of water. She filled the pot again for the morning's coffee.

They were all tasks Rafe normally did.

Usually Aubrey stayed behind in the tent to make up the bed.

She brushed her teeth and spit into the same bush. Then she carried the cook pot and water bag back to the tent.

She peeled off the rain gear and crawled into her mummy bag.

The tent was far too large for her now.

Empty and quiet and cold.

Rafe was up on the ridge alone.

It was too late now. It didn't matter. Nothing she could do would ever change it.

But she still had a part of him with her here.

She kept on her headlamp and reached for his pages.

He wrote at the end of every day. After all the camp chores were done. The tent was set up, dinner was cooking, and he'd sit and write about what they had done.

He was far more interested in that than Aubrey was. He kept track of their daily mileage. He liked to look at his maps.

He wrote down the meals they ate and which ones were great, which were awful. He wrote down the temperatures and the weather. He made lists of the birds and wildlife they saw. Whether they saw any other hikers. Where those people were from.

Aubrey started at the beginning, Rafe's notes from three nights ago.

She ran her fingers over the ink. His hand had written that. This was him.

Beautiful Aubrey...

The words caught her eye.

Beautiful Aubrey wore her fireweed colored top today.

Then he went on to write about the weather.

Her eyes skipped along the lines. Now all she wanted was to see her name.

Beautiful Aubrey sleeping in my arms this morning. Birds singing. Sun on the meadow. How am I so lucky? But if you ask, I guess it ruins it.

Then back to recording his dry, lengthy facts. Trail mileage. Weather. Food.

Aubrey made herself back up and read the entire entry.

You would have loved today. The high peaks and the blue, blue lakes. There isn't a soul up here except us. We saw a few deer before they got spooked and took off over a hill.

Beautiful Aubrey sleeping in my arms this morning. Birds singing. Sun on the meadow. How am I so lucky? But if you ask, I guess it ruins it.

Remember Coach Gleason? He was the fat one, not the mean one. Whenever one of us would actually get a run he always said, "It's better to be lucky than good."

You were good. I'm just lucky.

Miss you.

Aubrey stared at the words.

A chill swept across her skin.

It's to William.

Rafe's dead twin brother.

He still wrote to him.

Aubrey never knew.

She read on, and could see that she was right. Rafe wrote to his brother every night.

He talked about Aubrey. Talked as if William already knew her. Like they discussed her every day.

He was sharing his grown up life with his brother. Maybe even living it for them both.

You would have loved the rain...

I wish you could have seen this hawk...

Beautiful Aubrey brought me coffee in the tent...

That's who she always was. Not just plain Aubrey. Always Beautiful.

Sometimes it hurts how much I love her. I think you'd understand. You'd probably fight me for her.

And always the same two words at the end of every long record of the day.

Miss you.

Aubrey read all the pages a second time through. Rafe's letters to his brother.

Then she folded them neatly and sealed them back

in the waterproof bag. She stowed them in the top of her pack.

She turned off her headlamp and zipped herself into her solo sleeping bag. She wadded up her extra clothing and stuffed inside her hood for a pillow.

She lay awake listening to the rain beat against the tent.

The relentless rain that had made this day what it was.

The last day of her husband's life. The last day of her marriage. Maybe the last day she would ever be happy.

Aubrey sat back up inside her mummy bag. She unzipped the side to free her arms.

She opened the top of her backpack again and took out the bag with the pages.

There were still several blank loose leaf pages left. Rafe brought enough to write on for the entire trip.

Aubrey smoothed out a blank page on top of the stack and picked up Rafe's pen.

I miss you already. You were just here. Now you're gone.
I'm so sorry. I can't tell you how sorry.

You were the love of my life. I was so lucky to have you.
You made every single day of mine better.

You're on a mountainside now. It's rainy and cold. I have no idea what will happen to your body. I hope when I come back with people to help me get you down you'll still be wrapped up in your sleeping bag.

I'm going to read the map tomorrow. I'm going to read all your notes. I'll make sure to follow all the trails you already picked.

The weather was horrible today. The food was awful. My beautiful husband died. This was the worst day of my life.

But I still love you. I'll always miss you.

I hope you're with William now. I'm sorry I never got to meet him. Please tell him how much I loved his brother.

Goodbye, Rafe. I'm sorry I couldn't save you today.

But I loved you every single minute we got to spend together.

Aubrey clicked the pen closed.

Then clicked it back. Just two more words.

Miss you.

She sealed up the pages and then sealed herself back inside her sleeping bag.

It was a long hike out. She needed to be ready.

And she would have to start paying attention.

Then she could tell Rafe all about it tomorrow night.

THE RESCUE

1

Nick opened the latch at the front of his wood-burning stove and added more tinder to the firebox. He had already shoveled out the ashes from overnight and laid a new fire first thing, so the cabin was plenty warm, but the coffee wouldn't boil unless the fire was raging hot, so he kept nursing the flames and feeding them more.

The wind had been howling since he first woke up and shaking the walls of his one-room cabin. He wasn't worried. Miners had lived here before he had, and the place was still as solid as it ever was. Snow had been steadily falling for at least the last half hour, soft and puffy flakes at first, wetter and heavier now.

Avalanche snow. Not the kind of light snow he'd been seeing the past week. Sunny days, freezing nights, thaw-freeze-thaw—put a heavy new layer on top of a weak base like that, and a slab on one of these mountains was bound to break off and go.

The wind shook the cabin again and the dog groaned contentedly in answer. She scratched at one of her ears with a long hind foot and then settled back into her nap on the old wool rug beside the stove. She looked like a half-grown bear cub with all the thick brown fur she grew even thicker in the winters. It made it so she never seemed to mind the snow no matter how long they were out in it, but as soon as they were back inside she'd lie as close as she could to any fire, and at night whenever Nick shifted on his bed she'd shift right along with him to make sure she kept on getting all of his warmth.

The water was boiling now, so he added a few scoops of Folgers and tightened the lid back on the pot. He loved that smell: strong dark coffee on a cold morning. Loved the smell of butter melting on the skillet he had heating up right next to it.

He took out yesterday's pancake batter from his half-fridge and poured a pool of it onto the steaming skillet. He glanced at the dog, listened for a moment to the soft rumble of her snore, and poured a second small pancake for her.

The wind was blowing sideways now, and heavy snow hurtled itself against the cabin windows. A gust sent the bucket of cooling ash skittering across the wooden porch, and it made enough of a clatter that Bruna briefly opened one eye.

"Just a bit," Nick told her as he flipped over both pancakes. Then true to his word he dropped the finished pancake into her metal bowl and broke it into pieces with his spatula so it would cool faster and wouldn't burn her mouth.

Snow and wind blustered over the compound. There were newer cabins across the one-track road, and there were scientists inside them huddling in their long johns and blankets and fleece this and that, maybe worrying about whether they'd get to take all their measurements today, or else grateful for a day off.

Nick was grateful for the day off, too. A day off from all the yammerers asking him questions or trying to butter him up. "Are you the famous Nick Falls?"

"I'm Nick Falls," he'd tell them. "Don't know about famous." But he knew what they meant. Knew what they wanted to know.

They all wanted to hear the story.

How did he save those people?

2

When you've been in a place for fifty years, you know it in ways the day-tourists and the summer grad students and the winter scientists couldn't possibly understand.

Know it like you start knowing your own face through its changes, every brown spot, the wrinkles, the way your eyelids sink back deeper into their sockets the older you get. Not handsome, not ugly, just an old stump of a tree out in the woods, something reliable and recognizable, a way to measure your distances across the land.

And if you know how to be quiet—really deep down quiet, not just silent, holding your words back, but quiet like the bottom of a lake—then eventually you start to hear things.

Things that aren't from you.

You start looking at maps. Tracing the contours with the tips of your fingers, feeling the paper, then when you close your eyes—and you're *quiet*—you can feel the bumps of the land underneath the map. The rough rock faces. The soft mosses down in the clefts.

You can feel the way the land slopes here, how the edge of this map slips over to the next one, and it's windy over there now, and you can smell the sticky sap of a summer pine.

Nick had a drawer filled with maps, but that was before he could hear them. Back when they were just paper, just lines, just someone's idea of how to show what the land looked like.

Nick was out in that land every day. Taking measurements. Wind speed. Temperature. Rain. Snowfall. Recording when he saw the first robin and the first buds on the aspens in the spring.

He wanted to know the place. Know it *deep*. So he started keeping records long ago, just for himself.

Never dreaming they'd be valuable some day. That they would bring the scientists here all year round, to study the changes, to study his records. To prove what they already suspected about the way the world was going.

Back in the beginning, fifty years ago when he was twenty-four, Nick was supposed to be just the summer caretaker up here. The handy-man fix-it, whatever the scientists and students who lived in the row of rustic cabins for those few months of summer might need. Mouse trapping. Roof leaks. Nursing the fussy electricity.

But as the summer yellowed into fall, and the people all left, and the days got shorter and the nights longer, and it was just Nick and the vast mountains and the woods all around him, he found he had no desire to leave anymore. For what? Go back to what? Doing construction, drinking with his crew or drinking alone most nights, trying to find love, good luck with that—there was nothing.

Whereas here. Everything.

"You don't have to pay me any extra," he told the man who had hired him for just those few months. "I'll keep the place up all winter. Look after it. Just let me live here for free."

It was lonely sometimes that first winter. That was before he got a dog. Now Bruna was the fifth one in a row of the best dogs nature ever made. It always worked out that way, whether he got them from a friend of a friend or off the back of someone's pickup, *Pups4Sale*, when he went into town for groceries once a month.

Or, like with Bruna, a reject from one of the ranches down in the valley. Someone saw her listed in the want ads, under Farm Implements. *Ranch dog, $1.* They called up Nick, knowing he'd just lost old Blue, and he skied into town the next day, all eight miles, to meet the sonofabitch who would give up such a sweet and affectionate dog because she wasn't mean enough to herd.

As soon as they were clear of town traffic and any of the people, Nick slipped the collar off her neck and Bruna had been a free girl ever since. Trotting happily at Nick's side everywhere he went, as in love with him as he was with her.

It had been Bruna who woke him up that day. Told him to pay attention.

It was still dark out. In early February, sunrise didn't reach the cabin windows until after 7:00. Nick normally got up at 5:00 anyway, just to start the coffee and go back to bed to read.

But Bruna started whining around 4:00. "It's damn cold out there," he told her. He could hear the wind beating against the walls of the cabin. But Bruna didn't want to go out, she wanted him to listen to her, to pay attention.

She paced back and forth, her nails clicking against the wood floor.

Nick clicked on the light and watched her for a minute, wondering what was wrong. He couldn't hear anything but the wind outside. But maybe Bruna heard some animal. Nick listened harder.

Bruna sat then, close to the wall, and looked up toward the map hanging there.

There were maps all over the walls now, finally out of the drawers so that Nick could look at them every day. Contour maps of all the mountains surrounding the science station, showing the land that Nick and Bruna roamed all through the year.

Bruna kept panting, looking up at the map, whining at Nick.

"I don't know what you mean," he told her.

Bruna thumped her bushy tail against the wood floor.

She kept on like that for the next few hours. Through coffee, through pancake breakfast, through Nick checking the gauges and the thermometer and looking through the windows with the binoculars, writing down his notes on all the measurements and the observations he could make from inside the cabin. Delaying going out in the biting cold until the sun was well and truly up.

As the dark hours of the morning wore on, Bruna got more and more agitated. Pacing, nails *click click*, whining, coming over to Nick and licking his hand, sitting and thumping her tail.

He opened the door for her more than once, despite the snow blowing in. But Bruna didn't try to go out.

"I don't know what you *want*," Nick kept telling her. "What do you mean?"

Always she kept looking over toward that map.

3

Over the years, without ever trying, he'd gained a certain respect. Folks knew he was out here every day, every year, always watching and listening and learning.

A few times—more than a few—he'd fielded calls from Search and Rescue, asking for his help. Asking what he knew of the terrain this person had gone missing in. Asking if he saw any signs of rock falls or mountain lions or other hazards.

Any new avalanche slides.

Eventually they outfitted him with a radio so they could contact him in emergencies, and later a satellite phone that Nick got in the habit of carrying in his pack whenever he and Bruna went out to walk or ski the land.

He'd seen his share of dead bodies. It never got easier.

And Bruna, she hated it. She mourned about it. Whined and backed up and paced, ears flat.

"It's okay, girl," he'd tell her. "Nothing to be afraid of."

Some poor hiker or hunter or skier. It happened.

But Bruna would never be consoled. If Nick didn't move her on soon she'd start howling, letting the whole world know that something had gone very, very wrong.

Then she'd be out of sorts for days, like she took it personally. This person died, *on her land.* In her territory. She had failed somehow, ranch dog that she still was at heart. Like part of her own herd had been killed.

But it had been a while since Nick had gotten any calls from Search and Rescue, or accidentally come across a body. Over two years by then. It was a good run.

But now. Bruna was acting almost the same way. Ears back, pacing, whining.

Nick didn't want to believe it, but he was starting to.

She knew something.

She sensed something.

Maybe.

But to keep looking up at the map? What was that?

Did dogs do that? Could they even understand what a map was?

It couldn't be. But Nick had seen a lot of things that surprised him in the last fifty years, and so he had learned not to be skeptical if he might learn something new instead.

Out here in this world, his own world, he found it was better to listen. To go quiet. To watch. And then if he saw or heard something he knew was true, to believe.

"We'll go out there," he told the dog. Nick started putting on all the layers he would need, five of them in total. Bruna thumped her tail, watching him. She could see she had finally gotten through.

He took his usual winter gear, permanently in his pack: headlamp, emergency kit, an extra layer of clothing, and his avalanche beacon, shovel, and probe.

If Bruna was right, if she really meant to keep looking at that one particular map, then Nick knew where they had to go.

They set off.

It was an area about five miles from the science station, accessible off a road that was closed to winter traffic except snowmobiles.

Nick and Bruna came at it from the wilderness side, where there were no roads, where no snowshoe or ski had made a print or flattened the snow all winter. It wasn't a place Nick usually went until after the snow began to thaw. There were too many hidden dips where the dog might punch through, and he had learned with his first dog how hard it was to get them out.

Now that the sun was out, the day was looking better. The snow wasn't blowing so hard anymore, but it was still damn cold.

Bruna started out ahead of him, trudging as best she could through the deep snow, but Nick told her to wait and he skied out past her so she could follow in the track he made.

After just a few strides, he got into his rhythm and he didn't have to think about what his skis were doing, he could look around.

Sunlight glinted off the pure white landscape, sparkling like jewels. Heavy pillows of snow rested on the branches of the spruce and fir. Birds sang, same in the freezing temperatures as in the warmth of summer. There were rabbit prints at the edge of the forest, leading off into the trees.

Nick knew where the streams and gullies were, beneath the cover of snow, and he steered clear of them to always keep Bruna on solid ground.

He could hear the dog panting behind him, sometimes whining. She tried to go around him a few times, maybe impatient that he was going too slow, but Nick knew of a dog who broke its leg by falling into too deep of snow, and so he kept out in front of Bruna to make the track safe.

The snow had stopped falling for now. The wind had quieted down. The morning was brilliantly sunny and cold.

But the dog was more agitated than ever.

Finally she ignored his warning and raced out ahead of Nick. He could only pick up the pace and take longer, deeper strides, trying to keep up with her.

"Bruna!"

She barked. Not back at Nick, but ahead of her.

Up on the ridgeline, Nick could see four people. To be where they stood, they must have ridden snowmobiles part of the way, then climbed up the steepest part through the trees on their own.

Bruna barked. And kept barking. She paced, down here below at the base of the long, steep slope, so far from the people on top, Nick could barely see anything of them except their brightly-colored clothes.

The first skier took off.

The other three followed.

Bruna howled. Howled like she did when they came across dead bodies.

Nick felt a tingle all along his arms.

Something told him, but he was slow to believe it.

Take out the phone. Call them. Call them now.

Time was the only thing that mattered, in situations like this.

If this really was a situation.

Bruna laid back her head and howled again.

The mountain began to slip.

Nick fumbled with the clip on his pack. He finally released it from around his waist. He couldn't take his eyes off the mountain, off the snow, the way the slab was breaking off now, the way the whole mountainside was sliding—

But he had to find the satellite phone. Had to call. Had to get them coming, *now*. He was only one man. He needed a whole team. There were four people about to be buried.

"Bruna, NO!" She was running toward the path of the slide, in danger of being swept up in it just like the skiers. "BRUNA! COME!"

The dog howled and barked and ran a few more steps forward, but then she came back, thank God she came back, and Nick clutched a handful of her thick fur on the back of her neck, steadying himself, steadying her.

"Girl, you have to *wait*. I'm calling. Just wai—" Nick's voice hitched at the end, because Bruna looked up him then, her deep brown eyes so sad and bewildered, how could this happen? They were too slow! Too late! How could they let this happen?

"N-Nick Falls," he said when the dispatcher answered. He gave her his location. "Four skiers. All caught in an avalanche. All of them. Buried."

"We'll get there as soon as we can," she told him.

Too slow. Too late.

Time was all that mattered. In an avalanche, even if the massive force of it slamming into their bodies didn't kill them right away, snow would have filled their noses and mouths, cutting off any way to breathe.

Nick turned on his beacon to receiver mode.

But even if he was still young, even if he could still climb that mountainside, and even if his beacon picked up signals from four transmitters he assumed the skiers had on them—it would take too long. They would be buried too long. This wasn't going to work. Those people were dead.

But Bruna didn't know that. She was already racing up the slope, skidding, sliding, getting her feet solid again and running on.

"Bruna!"

She wouldn't listen.

There was no time. No time to do it the right way. To wait for help. To do what Nick had been taught to do.

Bruna had already stopped midway up the slope and was digging now, frantically digging.

Nick tried to cry out to her, but the sound clogged in his throat.

He cursed and started after her. The slope was solid enough. If this was it, if this was his day, if he died doing this, at least he died with his dog.

The skis were no good. He couldn't climb fast

enough with them on. So he unclipped them and continued in just his boots.

Right about then, a strange thing started happening with his eyes.

A kind of white blindness, sunlight reflecting off the snow, burning his eyes in a flash of pure white, making him see what he needed to see.

The snow was gone, for a flash of a moment.

He could see the four bodies, exactly where they landed.

The lowest one, the first skier who triggered the slide—that one was dead.

But the other three. There might still be a chance.

Bruna was right above one of them, continuing to frantically dig.

That one could live. But only if Nick got there in time.

From where he was, still climbing, it would take him minutes more to reach just that first body. The other two were further up. Maybe still alive right now, but for how much longer? There wasn't time to get to all of them and shovel them out enough to breathe.

He couldn't just uncover their faces. The snow was a vise squeezing their hearts and lungs. Digging out torsos took time. It took lots of shovels. Not just his own. It would be like trying to save the Titanic by bailing with a spoon.

Then that flash again. See the four bodies. *I see them. So what? What am I supposed to do? Help me!*

A thin line, tracing the slide path, noting the location of each skier beneath the snow.

Like a map.

Like an illuminated, living map.

Bruna was still digging. Digging so hard, so desperately, believing she could do it. She could save the person beneath.

Nick's breath caught in his lungs.

Goddammit, that dog. Nick knew, but he was afraid to believe. Even an open mind has its limits.

But if that goddamn dog knew something he didn't, what choice did he have but to go along?

None of this was natural. Starting with the dog waking up whining and going to the map.

Knowing something was going to happen a few hours later. Knowing with a certainty that Nick didn't have to understand before he believed.

He saw it again now, more clearly, because he allowed himself to see.

The lines of the map, drawing themselves on the snow.

The line from Bruna to the person beneath her. Then to the next skier up the hill. And the next.

Like someone laying track for Nick, making it easier, the way he did earlier for his sweet and desperate dog.

What was a map but a suggestion? A way of describing what somebody saw.

What did the mapmakers know of this land? They could only see the surface.

They didn't live in it, breathe it, take it into their minds and bodies and souls.

They had other maps to go make.

But Nick was part of this land, part of this mountainside, and his dog was part of this land, too. She knew her responsibility to save these people.

Nick had to help her in whatever way he could.

He couldn't worry about whether it would be true. He just had to try.

From where he stood, his boots braced against the slope, he raised his right arm, level with the view in front of him. Then he extended his index finger and started to trace the line he could still see illuminated on the surface.

A thin furrow started to appear. Like ski tracks digging into the snow.

Nick pressed down harder in the air. Thought it. Saw it.

He added his middle finger, to make a thicker line. Then his whole hand, scooping away the hard-packed ice crystals, then two hands, digging like Bruna.

His legs shook beneath him with the effort of holding his position, but he didn't dare move or try to climb higher.

He didn't need to. He could do what he needed from this distance, digging away at the air.

And Bruna was digging deeper because she could now, because Nick was clearing her a path.

She got down to the skier's face. Nick closed his eyes and he could see it. He used his fingers in the air to scoop out the snow in the young woman's mouth that had hardened with just a few breaths into a plug of ice.

Bruna was already racing up the hill to the next body. Digging.

I'll be there in a second! I'm coming.

Nick dug away the snow pressing on the woman's torso. He wasn't there beside her to do CPR or to give her his breath, but something else did that for him.

The young woman opened her eyes. Cried out. She was still trapped from the torso down, but by God, she was alive.

Nick raised his hands to the next location, where Bruna was already frantically digging a hole.

Step aside, girl. Let me help you.

Bruna barked and kept digging hard.

They worked together, it only took a minute, and the man beneath the snow was alive now, too.

Just one more. Bruna struggled mightily up the slope. She was tiring. Tired. Nick could feel how exhausted she was.

He made a track for her. He knew she wouldn't

come back to him if he called. She had work to do and she would do it, do it until she was done.

He traced a furrow for her in the snow. Helped her reach the highest body.

Then with his hands digging again in the air—this impossible piece of magic, but there it was—Nick and Bruna worked together, clearing the man's throat so he could breathe, lifting the heavy snow from the skier's chest, catching life before it left him and settling it back into his frame.

Nick could hear snowmobiles in the background. Help was coming. But it would still take time for the rescuers to climb to the top of the ridge, then carefully ski their way down.

Bruna had an idea and there was no keeping her from it. She half-slid, half-ran down the steep and dangerous slope to where the lowest body lay, already dead beneath the snow.

She was no less frantic. Not taking her time because she sensed the life was gone. She whined and howled and dug like a creature possessed.

Nick couldn't bear to stand by and only watch, even though he knew the dog would be inconsolable once she discovered the death underneath.

It's okay, girl. We'll get him. But let me do it. You've done enough.

The first rescuer was up on the ridge now. The others were soon there, too. They had the right equipment. They had enough people to do the job. Many shovels. It would go better from now on.

It was strange to see the living bodies still half submerged inside the snow. They might have broken bones. Internal injuries. But that wasn't for Nick to know or to try to fix.

All he cared about now was the futile desperation of his Bruna, howling and digging out the snow. Nick wasn't sure if he could still do it with the rescuers watching. Or whether he should. It was going to be too hard to explain.

But he couldn't watch Bruna fight the snow any longer. Nick raised his two hands and he helped her dig. If anyone up the hill saw what happened, he would have to accept that. Some things were too important to try to hold yourself back.

When the head was cleared, and Nick scooped the snow out of the young man's mouth, Bruna howled in her mournful way. So Nick kept going, digging the torso free. Bruna bounced and barked on the edge of the hole.

From where he stood, Nick couldn't exactly see what went on, but the top half of Bruna disappeared into the hole.

He dug out more, and her whole body fit inside it.

She was licking the young man's face. He wasn't sure how he knew, but he knew.

The face was a vivid, shocking blue. The air had

long stopped moving inside the skier's lungs. It was hopeless. But Bruna wouldn't give up.

She was made to save and protect, and she did.

Farm Implement, $1.

A digger, a herder, a machine now that wouldn't stop.

And by God, if she didn't do it.

By God, if that young man didn't open his eyes.

Nick let out a shout. He pointed. He couldn't believe it himself, but he knew what he knew.

The rescuers were all there on the slope now, shovels at work, and two of them broke away to go dig out the skier Nick had known was once dead.

"Come on, girl. Bruna! Come away now. Good girl, good girl."

Nick felt drained of all energy. He could feel it in his dog, too. Bruna limped across the side of the snow path. But her tail was wagging. She knew what she had done.

Nick knelt in the snow, arms wide open to receive her. The dog continued making her slow and limping way toward him. Then she folded herself inside. "Good girl, good girl. Best girl."

Nick buried his face in her fur.

4

She was older now, made older by her efforts. She might not last as long as she otherwise would. At seven she had the slow, careful ways of a dog twice her age. Nick had to accept that. She had done her job.

If she spent her days now more in front of the fire than out on the land, Nick would do the same. He was getting older, too. Maybe older than he should feel by now, but he didn't mind that so much. He and his dog were traveling the same road.

There was a deep down tired that Nick could feel in his bones, all the way through to the marrow. Maybe he and Bruna both left something of themselves on the slide path that day. They spent what they had, and that was all right.

For whatever reason, they'd been allowed to save

four people that day. But it seemed they were meant to do it only once, and never again. Nick doubted either of them could ever summon up the energy again, even if they tried. And that was all right, too.

In the days and weeks after, here in the deep quiet of his cabin, Nick spent a lot of time going over what he saw.

He would be a fool to doubt any part of it. Even if no one else would ever believe it or could possibly explain it.

He wrote it all down in his notes. Everything that happened. For some open-minded scientist to find in Nick's papers after he was gone, to read and ponder whether what happened might somehow be true.

Like some ancient sailor logging all the mythical creatures that he saw, out in the vast mysteries of the sea. Leave it to someone in later times to name them whales and octopi and dolphins. Leave it to the scientists to call them real.

Nick and Bruna were just explorers. Out in the unknown. Walking this land and learning what secrets it held.

Sometimes Nick still placed his palm flat against a map on his wall, closed his eyes, and let himself feel it. Feel the land and the rocks beneath the paper, feel the land coming through to his skin.

It wasn't for him to understand. But it sure was his to believe.

The dog groaned contentedly beside the wood-burning stove. She shifted her weight, found a more comfortable position.

Nick reached down and scratched her behind her ear. He felt such a love for her he couldn't describe it.

A man has a connection with a dog, there's nothing else like it. It's the most precious thing in the world. But dogs never live as long as you want them to. You have to take what they give while you can.

"Good girl," he whispered. "Best girl."

She was the last dog he would ever have, the last one he ever needed. They would walk out this long, slow road together now to the end. And that was all right with him.

HOME DEER

HOME DEER

I understand not everyone would agree with me. I don't care.

People have weird ways of trying to make it right.

They pray over their kill. They thank it. They say words they've read in old Native American texts. *I honor you, Brother Deer, Brother Elk.* And they still kill it. Makes absolutely no sense to me.

This summer I signed up for plant camp. Supposed to be a week of camping out in the woods, walking around with our notebooks while the Earth Mother herbalist from our little mountain town taught us which plants we could eat, which ones we could use to make special tinctures and salves, which ones would poison us.

The kind of thing Phil would have scoffed at.

Would have called witchy, learning how to make my witch's brew.

That's right, Phil. Could have saved you, if I knew a few more things.

The herbalist was natural all the way. Didn't believe in washing very much. Very … musky, let's say. Fragrant. Not shy about her B.O.

Hair in her armpits, hair on her legs. Kind of exciting to see, frankly, since I was raised to shave every day ever since junior high. "You want your legs as smooth as a dolphin," my mother used to say. And hairy armpits were just for European women, not for good old Americans.

Natural, groovy, peace-loving herbalist, right? So of course I assumed she was a vegetarian.

Yet first night's dinner, she wanted to teach us a ceremony.

She led us into the woods where she had a little pig tied up there. Squealing. Even in the summer it gets cold at night. And that poor animal was cold and frightened.

No, I told her. HARD no.

I won't even go into it.

I turned around, packed up my clothes and sleeping bag and tent, and I set out on foot. I'd carpooled out there with one of the other students I met online, but she was staying. They were all staying.

I walked all seven miles back to town, in the dark, over narrow twisty mountain roads. I didn't care.

"But we do it in a sustainable way," the herbalist told me about killing and cooking the pig. She said I was crazy to walk home, just wait until morning. "And we sing over it. Pray over it. It's actually very spiritual."

The things people tell themselves.

So I've had to study on my own. That's fine. I'm a good learner. Once I get onto a subject, I go deep. Insanely deep. I follow the bread crumbs, one book to another, one teacher to another, and I sponge it all up. Night and day. For months.

And that's how I found some ceremonies of my own.

But that comes in later. Let me tell this right.

I live in a quiet little subdivision cut into the side of some low hills, with some bigger mountains rising behind us.

Beautiful in every season. Covered in wildflowers in the summer, plenty of aspens to turn yellow and red in the fall, lovely in winter and spring with snow on the peaks and bright blue skies above. The kind of place you'd see on a postcard or a calendar, and I get to live here every day.

I'm not from here. I grew up in the desert, in a city, where everything was brown. The first year Phil brought me here, my eyes practically watered from seeing all the green.

"Think you'll like it here?" he asked, grinning at me. Because of course I loved it right away. It was a childhood dream come true.

That plays in, too. Just wait a minute.

Phil wasn't everything I wanted, but he was a lot of it. Very manly man. A smoker, not great. A hunter, but back then I didn't mind it like I do now. Back then I had never seen a hunt and didn't know what it would be like.

An outdoorsman in every way. And he turned me into an outdoorswoman. I took to it like static to electricity. Learned to hike, fish, ski. Camped out. Backpacked. Did all of it.

He taught me how to shoot. Pistol, shotgun, rifle. And it was fun. I was a natural. Steady hand, good eye.

And it fit an image I had of myself, you know? Good sport. Hardy. A good companion. The kind of wife a man would want with him all the time, not someone he'd leave behind to go off with the boys.

I sucked it up, even when it wasn't what I wanted. Like the time his friend Randy bought a tag to hunt elk, but Phil didn't for one reason or another. Phil volunteered the two of us to help Randy haul out the elk if he shot one.

Randy shot one.

We met him up on the autumn hillside. Blue sky, yellow aspens, everything as potentially beautiful as always.

But ugly that day. Tragic.

I looked down at that poor animal. The light gone from his eyes. And Phil's friend Randy whooping it up like it was the biggest accomplishment of his life. "Look at that rack!" Phil whooping right along with him. Smiling over at me, expecting me to do the same.

Experienced hunters know that an elk or a deer isn't a one-piece problem. You don't carry out the whole animal. An elk is as big as a horse.

I won't go into it. But I was there for the … separation, let's call it, and I hauled out my portion of the meat in a big black garbage bag, making Phil so proud that his wife was such a sturdy little thing, look at Dorothy go, never complaining.

But that was the beginning of the end for me.

It was the beginning of the end for Phil, too. He was some years older than me, and even though he was fit for his age, it puts a strain on the heart to hike those rugged mountains hauling all that weight. Then hiking back up and doing it again. Like I said, an animal that big isn't a one-piece problem.

If I'd known what I know now, I could have done something to help him. I could have made Phil a special brew—yes, Phil, a witch's brew, go ahead and call it that, my *potion*—and it would have mended the strain on his heart right then, that same night.

But instead it was like a little muscle tear that makes you limp just a little, and then the next time you try to run on it, suddenly your leg goes out and you're down.

Only with your heart, you don't limp, you just slow down. You feel tired. Your breathing is a little irregular.

And then one day, that's it. Down. Out.

I've been a good widow to him. I keep his memory alive. I still love him. I think about him all the time.

I still live in our house, up here in the mountains, even though my family is still back in the desert, in the city, ready to fold me back in.

I have things to do here. Things to make. Things to try.

After the walk home from plant camp, I sat in my living room that night resting my sore feet, and I thought about what I really want.

More. I wanted more. More, even, then what I thought I might learn from that Earth Mother herbalist.

So I began my studies. I let my conscience be my guide. I didn't have to answer to anybody, didn't have to impress anybody anymore with being any particular way.

I was going to raise myself from scratch.

I learned about plants. I learned about weather. I learned about seasons and cycles of the moon. I cooked and concocted things in the privacy of my own little kitchen.

If I sometimes heard Phil ridiculing me, I took it in good humor.

"That's right," I'd tell him out loud. "This one will cure any headache. Wait and see."

I started treating some of the ladies in the neighborhood. Women are always so much more receptive.

Cuts, aches, pains, they started bringing them all to me.

Then the broken toe. Healed that one. The sprained ankle. Did that. I pretended it was the salves and the wraps, because people aren't always comfortable with the truth. As long as my heart was always in the right place, just wanting to help people with my new skills, I decided they didn't need to know all the ins and outs.

Summer was nearly over. It's always so short around here. By mid-August the aspen leaves were already starting to turn yellow.

By then, I had learned one or two special ceremonies.

You just have to know where to look for knowledge. Sometimes it's in books that are a hundred years old.

You just have to be patient. And curious. And persistent. I've been blessed with all three of those all my life.

So by the time August passed, and then September, I was ready for hunting season in October.

When the weather turns cold, the deer start coming

down off the highest hills. They walk through our subdivision. They graze on our properties.

"It's not called grazing," Phil corrected me the first time I said it. "Deer browse."

I can say whatever I want now. I make up my own rules. Deer graze.

There was a little family I saw every dawn and every dusk. Two mamas, two babies, and one huge, magnificent buck. The kind of rack that would have had Phil and his buddy Randy hyperventilating.

That buck had earned his antlers. I didn't know until Phil told me, but deer shed their antlers every year and grow new ones. That's why the youngest males have just little spikes in the beginning. The older bucks grow bigger and bigger racks every year, until they're past their prime, and then their racks get smaller every year. I'm sure there's a metaphor in that.

You can go out in the mountains in the spring and find the antlers just lying on the ground. There are places in town that will pay you to bring them in so that some artisan can make furniture out of them, like chandeliers and coat racks and headboards for tourists who want to feel rustic.

There are some hunters that even sell the whole stuffed heads with their staring plastic eyes and their big impressive racks so that some guy somewhere can mount it in his den and tell people he shot it himself.

One of the stores in town decorates a big elk head every year for Christmas, with strings of lights across all the horns. So disrespectful. That magnificent old elk would have preferred being alive and free, not covered in blinking lights above the storefront like a tacky lawn ornament.

But I had my little family of deer taking their time grazing across my property twice a day, weaving among the sage bushes, snacking on the vegetation. Then they'd head up a few streets higher in the subdivision and bed down at my neighbor's house, right next to their garage, every afternoon.

The way Phil explained it, the deer migrate every year, coming off the highest slopes down to our neighborhood where they hang around for a few days, *browsing*, then they keep on moving down to lower country as part of their annual migration route.

"But you'd never shoot one of those deer we see here," I said as I watched a buck strolling through our sage early one morning.

"'Course not," Phil said. "Those are our home deer." I remember him smiling tenderly and kissing me on the cheek.

The things people tell themselves. The things hunters tell their tender-hearted wives.

But it gave me a view of how the whole thing works. What the deer do. How hunters think.

So comes mid-October. The opening of hunting season, first period lasting nine days from Saturday to the following Sunday.

Parks and Wildlife gives out a limited number of deer tags in our area, but anyone can come from anywhere and buy an elk tag right over the counter.

The thought, Phil said, is that elk are really hard to find. So it's no skin off Parks and Wildlife to say anyone from Pennsylvania or Oklahoma or Texas can come right in and give it a try. Please pay your seven hundred dollars, thank you very much.

But deer. Deer are easy. Deer are just trotting across the road when you're driving out to get groceries.

Deer are ambling across people's properties every dawn and dusk, driving their dogs crazy who are stuck inside barking at them from the window.

But those are my deer. My home deer. Each and every one of them.

I've got good equipment. Some of it was Phil's, some of it was mine from when he was setting me up as the good-sport sturdy little wife.

I've got full hunter's orange: bright orange baseball cap, long-sleeved orange shirt, thick orange vest with pockets for bullets, all of them making me visible from at least a mile away.

I've got a Browning A-Bolt 30.06 rifle with a Leupold scope. Very competent firearm.

I look the part. For a brief period, I was the part. And I think it gives all those hunters from Pennsylvania and Oklahoma and Texas a little chuckle when they see me hiking up a ridge, all decked out, my expensive competent rifle slung on a sling across my back.

All of us lighting the pre-dawn darkness with headlamps strapped to our foreheads.

One of them might tip his hunter's cap to me. "Ma'am."

Some of them look suspicious. Where's my man? What am I doing up there all alone?

Some might look at me as an opportunity. Except I have that rifle and as far as they know I'm ready to use it.

I sing a little, low under my breath.

Sing words. Sing my ceremony. Quietly and continuously.

They don't appreciate the noise. Think it spooks the deer off. But I keep on hiking past them, keep on heading up the mountain to the next ridge, and they figure I'll be out of earshot soon enough.

But I've laid my trap. Laid my bread crumbs. They don't even know.

I sprinkle a little this and that. Shake a little tincture out of a bottle.

My witch's brew. My potions. My weapons.

There are laws on the books here and in a lot of

other states saying it's a crime to interfere with a hunter.

A crime to try to chase away game. Or to interfere with a hunter's shot.

A crime to harass some poor innocent rifle-toting predator who has paid good money to kill a docile and majestic beast.

But I've never been caught. And I won't be.

They might feel a little sick. Just a swishing low in their gut. And their vision blurs a little. Like they still haven't drained out all the whiskey they drank in camp the night before.

They feel tired. Natural, since they were up at four in the morning to be out here on this ridge with their headlamps in the dark before the deer are stirring for the day.

They have some muscle weakness. Their legs don't work exactly right.

They feel a little off-balance. All part of the brew.

But they wouldn't know it was me, hiking past them singing a little song. It's not like I gave them spiked coffee or a muffin or anything they can pinpoint.

The problem with trying to warn off the deer is I might actually chase them right into some hunter's view. Backfire. I might kill what I'm trying to save.

But there's a ceremony for that, too. One I found in

a half-page reference in a book I bought from a used book site. Something donated probably when kids cleaned out their parents' or grandparents' old farmhouse. The kind of old text that people who used to live close to the land knew very well spoke the truth.

The opposite of killing something while you tell it, *I honor you, Brother Deer, Brother Elk.*

The kind of ceremony that says, *I protect you with my magic. I honor you with your life.*

When I was a little girl, back in the dry brown city desert, I used to read obsessively from this book someone gave me for Christmas.

A book about a little girl who lived in a cottage at the edge of the woods, and every day she would go out in the forest and talk with her animal friends.

Woodland friends like chipmunks and squirrels and deer. She sang to them. They loved her. She loved them.

In the autumn when the hunters came, she hid them in a magical cave. She stood watch every dawn and dusk. She made sure all the deer got away.

Her father wanted to kill animals to feed his family, but the little girl would never let him. She didn't cry, she didn't beg, she just made sure she protected her friends with her secret magic.

A book like that makes an impression. On me, anyway. Some other little girl might forget it, go on to reading grown-up novels and textbooks and fashion magazines, but I am still that same little girl in my heart.

I found the magic that protects my friends.

My home deer. My home elk. Anything these hunters think they might kill.

I get tired, sure. Those are early mornings, hiking in the dark, hauling my heavy rifle. And I'm out there all day long, every day of the hunting periods, until after dusk when I hike back down.

But the hunters I pass, the ones I sing my special song to, the ones who catch a whiff of my witchy potion—they're a lot more tired than I am.

They surprise themselves by wanting to lie down in the frosty grass and take a little nap. Even more surprised when they wake up hours later, not feeling so great, just wanting to sleep some more.

If the snow falls, as it often does this time of year, they might find themselves cozy underneath it, sleeping their heat away. I haven't seen it happen yet. I just assume that's possible.

I'm new to this. But I'm learning. I'm practicing. As anyone who wants to master a skill must.

Hunting season lasts into December. There are both rifle and archery seasons. I get lots of practice. I'm getting quite good.

So far, not a single animal lost.

So far, I'm the little girl with her magic cave.

What would I do if some hunter slipped through and shot one of my woodland friends?

There are ceremonies for that, too.

Not all of them very gentle when it comes to the hunter.

But I won't go into that.

I'll just say that in my own way I'm praying over them and singing over them, and just like the Earth Mother herbalist tried to convince me, it's all actually very spiritual.

I honor you, Brother Hunter.

It just depends on who you're rooting for, the predator or the prey.

Phil wouldn't have approved of any of it, but I wouldn't have told him if he was still alive. He just would have found himself strangely unable to get off a clear shot. His hand would shake. His vision would blur.

His sturdy, sporty wife who was out there with him in her hunter orange and sporting her own rifle would have patted her man on the shoulder. She would have cracked open the thermos and poured them both some coffee. She would have unpacked the peanut butter and jelly sandwiches that she made. For whatever reason, she wasn't serving roast beef anymore.

"It's okay," she would have told her husband. "Better luck tomorrow." Or "Better luck next year."

But the home deer would be safe in this vast backyard that reaches all the way to the top of the mountains.

And the grown up little girl in the cottage at the edge of the woods would make sure they stayed safe in her magical forest for a long, long time.

THE GOLD HUNTER

THE GOLD HUNTER

It was precarious, slope side, but Walter didn't dare move him. There was a gash on the back of the kid's head, about four inches long, bloody and already swelling.

He looked about twenty. Tall, strong-looking, but a sick paleness to his skin now. Five, maybe ten minutes in already, and the boy still hadn't woken up.

There was a squall hanging over them. One of those surprise August storms that looks like it will just be more rain—expected—but that suddenly turns into blinding and dangerously cold summer sleet.

There was a saying up here in the mountains: Don't like the weather? Wait ten minutes. It will change.

Tourists were always getting caught out. Day-hikers, campers, ambitious through-hikers on the Continental Divide.

Even old hands, like Walter, could still misjudge it. In the twenty years he'd lived up here, there wasn't a month when he hadn't been snowed on at least once. Hell, it even snowed one year during the Fourth of July parade. That made the papers.

But sleet like this was different. It landed hard and wet and brutal, chilling you faster than you could get your rain gear on. And it made the rocks on the trail slick. In their frenzy to get someplace else, maybe back to their vehicles or to some imagined shelter, people hurried, trying to outrun it somehow, but it only made them careless.

A mistake just like this one. Walter was on his way back down the mountain when he heard the yell. More like a quick shout of surprise. Then the sound of rock-fall. A body thudding, thumping down the hill.

"Hello?" he called out once, twice.

His hearing was still good, even with the wind roaring in his ears, so he took the lack of response for what it was. A body had fallen and the person was knocked out. Optimistically, that was all it was.

Maybe it was best the kid still hadn't woken up for now. He had a broken leg that Walter might be able to set—the bone hadn't broken the skin, but Walter could see the extra knee-looking protrusion halfway down the kid's lower leg—and his right shoulder was jacked forward, a knob in front where there shouldn't be one. Dislocated, likely. Walter probably couldn't do anything about that. The muscles all around it would already be contracting hard, and one man didn't have the strength to roll it back into place. It was what it was.

He didn't know very sophisticated medicine, but he'd been around enough injuries in the backcountry and on the job site to know which he might be able to at least stop from getting worse.

Walter cinched the hood of his rain coat tighter under his chin, and went to work on straightening the leg. Pull out, give it some traction, then gently try to slip it back into line.

He sweated, even in the cold sleet, and it took a lot more time and strength than he expected. But eventually the extra knee disappeared, back into the smooth natural line of the leg.

"Damn," Walter mumbled, wiping the chilled sweat from his face. But the young man showed no reaction.

That was trouble. He had been out too long by now.

Walter rubbed his fist against the kid's chest. "Hey. *Hey.*"

But nothing. Just the same shallow rise of the ribcage, showing that the guy was still breathing.

Walter sat down on the wet slope and took a minute or two to gather his wits.

They were about two and a half miles from the

trailhead, where Walter's old white Jeep waited. He assumed the kid had left a vehicle of some kind there, too.

Two and a half miles wasn't very far. If it were just Walter now, he would keep hiking out, despite the cold and the sleet, and at a minimum find dry shelter inside the Jeep while he waited this out.

The road to the trailhead was already challenge enough to drive, even in regular August conditions. There was a stream crossing about halfway to the road, and it was already deep enough to wet the belly of the Jeep.

Add more rain to it, like this, and the engine would get swamped.

And even then, if Walter could make it to the road, the road itself was iffy. There were mudslides and washouts all the time. He might dodge them, get out just in the nick, or he might find himself perfectly timed to be buried just as some mudslide broke.

Again, if it was just him…

The kid was maybe six foot. He outweighed Walter by at least forty or fifty pounds. All of it muscle and bone. Walter was puny in comparison. He wasn't getting this body out on his own.

The kid had to stand. Walk out. Or be brought out by a team.

But no one was coming for him right now, that much was sure. No cell service up here, not missing long enough for someone expecting him at home—if there was anyone—to wonder if maybe something happened.

Of course there was someone. It wasn't like with Walter. No one would miss him until Monday at the earliest, when he didn't show up for work.

But a Saturday night for this kid? There would people who missed him for sure. Maybe a sweetheart, his parents, somebody.

Unfortunately, in the way of people, even if they were worried, they'd doubt themselves. They'd wait longer. It would probably be nightfall before they called dispatch, and then who knew how fast anything could happen.

It depended on the weather. Search and Rescue had protocols of their own. They wouldn't risk their people in dangerous conditions to come look for someone who had misjudged it himself.

If the road was washed out. If mud and rock blocked the way. If the sleet kept going, if temperatures dropped even more—probably more ifs than Walter could even guess at.

Damn it. *Damn* it. This wasn't going to resolve itself any time soon.

But meanwhile the kid was breathing. His heart was still pulsing at the side of his neck. That was something.

It *was* something.

Now Walter had to think.

Options:

He could drag the guy down the hill, onto the trail.

And then what?

Then nothing. He had no better way of keeping the kid warm or dry down there than up here. Plus in dragging him, he might make the dislocated shoulder worse, and there was the gash at the back of his brain to think of. Head injuries were the worst.

There had been a car accident on Highway 550 a few years ago, right as Walter was coming back from a job. Three people in a sport ute.

The driver, a kid in his twenties, like this one, had cuts all over his face and arms from ramming into the windshield.

But it was the twist in his shoulder from hitting the steering wheel that kept him screaming like he was being tortured. A dislocated shoulder, like this one. So the rescuers, like anybody, were paying attention to him, trying to make him better so he'd stop screaming.

While meanwhile the girl who was a passenger just sat calmly in her seat. Staring ahead, alive, awake, but out of it.

Turned out blood was leaking in her brain—into it or out of it, Walter wasn't sure of the details—but he heard from one of his buddies that she died right there at the scene, after Walter and all the other drivers had been waved through.

"It's the quiet ones you have to worry about," his friend said. "Not the screamers."

What if this kid died on him, just like the girl did?

Died because there was nothing Walter could do about it. If the boy's brain was bleeding or leaking—what was Walter supposed to do to stop it?

But the kid was alive now, his skin warm inside his jacket, despite the driving sleet.

Maybe that was the only thing Walter should worry about: Keep this body warm.

The kid had good gear. A thick yellow Patagonia—Pata-gucci, some called it—outer shell made of proper Gore-Tex, not some knock off.

An Arc'Teryx pack, Black Diamond hiking sticks. Lowa boots. Mammut hiking pants.

Like someone had dressed him for an outdoor photo shoot. But the gear wasn't new off the rack. This kid had obviously worn it for a season or two. He wasn't a beginner. Or at least his clothing wasn't.

Walter hadn't wanted to move the kid any more than he had to, not on this slope, but now he carefully undid the pack straps and slid them off the guy's arms —mindful of that knob of shoulder joint so wickedly out of place, the outline of it visible beneath the front of the yellow jacket—so he could look inside the pack. See if there might be some help there.

Pretty standard. A water bladder and hose, a few snack bars—they'd want those—sunscreen, an aluminum box with just an empty sandwich bag inside, black Patagonia rain pants that the kid must have thought were too much bother to put on.

Too late now. No way Walter was disturbing that broken leg.

But he laid the pants on top of the kid's lower half, to at least do something against the sleet.

Maybe it was Walter's imagination, but there seemed to be less of it now.

Less sleet, but also less light.

He planned on being out of here by now.

Driving his Jeep back in plenty of light. But even though the sun was still technically up, and wouldn't set for maybe another hour, the clouds were making the whole sky dark with early dusk.

Walter didn't have a flashlight with him. The kid didn't either.

That was stupid of both of them.

What did he have? A small pack with just the essentials, since carrying the metal detector was already a chore.

He could tuck the base of it into the belly of his pack, with the handle sticking up out of the top, banging against the back of his skull more than he liked.

But carrying it in his hands on these tricky slopes and thin, rocky trails was no better. So he kept just his rain gear and some water in the pack, and always planned on being out just a few hours, then getting home before he was hungry.

Where he went was always the same. He could get there and back in his sleep.

Even in the dark, if it came to that. But that was if he was alone.

He wasn't. There was no question that he would stay with the boy. No question at all. Leaving him here, alone, wet and cold and unconscious, was not even a momentary thought.

But Walter had no intention of spending the night on this slope, freezing to death from the sleet right along with him.

There had to be some way.

The sleet was definitely easing up now. It was more like a thin rain. Still colder than a summer storm should be, but what should be didn't matter.

Walter opened his pack again. Was he really so stupid that there was nothing to help them at all? Just a bag of his finds for the day, jostling against each other, making their thin and pebbly sound.

He hadn't been up here for a few weeks. It was a good haul. Probably about fourteen hundred dollars' worth.

Not that it would matter if they found him dead from stupidity on the side of this hill, or if this kid died and Walter made it out.

He didn't want to have to tell that story. Not to anyone else, not to himself.

It was time to do something. Anything but just sit here and wonder.

He might have at least some gray tone of light for another forty-five minutes, maybe an hour. After that, pitch black. So the time to get moving was now.

He jostled the kid's good arm. "Hey. Can you hear me now? HEY."

Walter ground his knuckles into the young man's chest again. He'd seen that in a movie, a way of testing whether someone unconscious was really faking it.

The kid moaned. Just a soft murmur coming from his throat, but it was sound. The first sound the guy had made.

"Hey!" Walter answered, encouraged. He rubbed his knuckles hard in a circle again. The kid moaned. They were getting somewhere. Although he still hadn't opened his eyes.

Walter's mind raced ahead of him. If they could somehow walk out. Get to the cars. Get warm. Maybe even drive out of here.

There was the broken leg to deal with. Walter might have set the bones back in the right line, but they wouldn't support any weight. The minute he got the kid to his feet, the bones would likely split apart again.

But if Walter could set the leg somehow. Do it the

old-fashioned way, like the cowboys in movies. Use sticks and strips of clothing.

He scanned the hillside around them. Plenty of downed branches. In a quick burst of ambition, Walter pushed to his feet and started collecting all of them he could find.

When he had an armful, he came to his senses. He didn't need twenty, he just needed two, right? One on each side of the leg. The right width and length, though, and evenly matched. He dropped the wood and started sifting through it. Found a reasonably likely pair.

Clothing. He had nothing extra on himself. What about the kid? There were the rain pants. Maybe Walter could cut those up. He did have a pocket knife. He always kept one in his pack, for no particular reason except it seemed like it would be good to have one if you needed it.

He had never made a splint before. But he had an idea what it should look like. A long stick on the outside of the leg to brace it from about the ankle up to the mid-thigh, and another stick on the inside, from the ankle up to the groin.

Then strips of fabric wrapped around them and tied to hold them in place. Maybe one at the thigh, another above the knee, another below the break. Maybe.

Once Walter started laying out the two branches,

he wasn't so sure. They were knobby and bent. Maybe too thin around. He didn't want to get this wrong. But he also didn't want to take too long figuring it out. Not while he still had some light and he might somehow get this kid out of here.

Another moan. Maybe because Walter was bothering that leg. But a moan was good. A moan might lead to awake.

"Hey! Can you hear me?"

But still nothing more.

The rain was a persistent, annoying factor now, but not as hard and cold as before. Walter's fingers felt clumsy, though. He paused and blew on them to warm them.

During that pause he caught sight of the kid's hiking poles.

Awfully thin around, but also perfectly straight.

And adjustable.

Walter opened the lock mechanism on one of them and tested how short he could make it. Then he matched it to the stick he had planned for the outside of the leg. Maybe the two of them together would do the job.

He made the adjustment on the second pole and added it inside the leg.

Then he examined the rain pants, tried to plan out his cuts before he made them. This would be his only chance to get that right.

He cut lengthwise down one of the legs, cutting six long strips that were thick enough that they wouldn't dig into the kid's skin when he tied them. Walter only cut up one leg, in case it turned out he did it wrong. He would still have the rest of the pants as fallback.

He blew on his fingers again. He was nervous. But what did it matter if he didn't do it perfect? He was all this kid had.

Walter laid out his strips in six places across the leg. He hoped the kid would stay oblivious after all, just for a little while longer.

Because he had to pick up the leg to do this. Starting at the ankle, lifting the leg high enough to slip the strip underneath it and wrap the sticks and poles tightly into place.

By the second strip, Walter realized he should do the lifting just one more time. So he rested the kid's boot on his thigh and quickly slipped all the other strips underneath the leg, all the way up to mid-thigh, then he gently lowered the foot to the ground.

Now it was just factory work. Position the sticks and poles, tie. Position, tie.

The kid still wouldn't be able to put much weight on that leg, but at least it might not buckle beneath him.

Especially with Walter holding him up and helping him walk.

If the kid woke up enough to do it.

Another moan then. A slight movement of the head.

"Oh, don't do that," Walter told him. "Keep it steady." He pressed his palm to the kid's forehead to keep him from jostling it and maybe making the head injury worse.

So how was Walter going to get him on his feet and down this slope without jostling it even more?

Night was coming on. The rain was just a spit now. But the ground was still slick beneath them.

Walter blew out a breath. This whole thing was impossible.

The kid moaned again.

"Hey," Walter said. "I'm here."

The eyes opened slightly, just slits. They blinked and opened a little wider.

"I'm Walter. Can you talk?"

"Mmm." Then the pain seemed to hit the kid all at once. His head, his shoulder, his leg.

He started panting. Sweat beaded on his pale face. His forehead wrinkled. His eyes winced.

"I know," Walter said. "It all hurts. You took a bad fall. I'm trying to get you out."

The kid opened his eyes again, part way. "How … bad."

No sense in lying. "Broken leg, I'm working on that. Dislocated shoulder, I can't really do anything about that right now. And maybe a concussion, or … anyway, you've been out for quite a while."

Walter didn't want to say it was a head injury. That the kid's brain might be bleeding. He wasn't a doctor. He didn't know.

The kid reached with his good arm and clutched his injured shoulder. He hissed in a breath. Then he felt for the back of his head. Felt the lump and the gash there. Winced.

Sweat was still slicking the kid's face. Walter thought it was best to get him talking.

"What's your name?"

The kid closed his eyes for a moment, as though thinking, maybe trying to remember.

"Matt."

"Okay," Walter said. "Good. Anyone know you're out here?"

Again, it took a long time to answer.

Finally, a mumbled, "Yeah."

The kid—Matt—looked like he might be going out again. Walter needed him to stay awake.

"It's almost dark. We have to get you up. No one's coming for us. Understand?"

Matt's eyes slitted open again, barely, and a thin smile lifted the corners of his mouth.

"Rescue me?"

"Yeah, I'm trying to rescue you," Walter said. "But you're going to have to put up with a lot of pain. You got that? I'm not kidding. But if you don't, you're going to die."

It was a strange kind of pep talk, but it seemed like the only way to do it. The kid was rolling in and out now like a drunkard. It reminded Walter of trying to get his old man off the couch and into bed.

"You're young and strong," Walter said. "You can take this. It's going to hurt more than you can stand. But then it'll be over, and I can take you to the hospital. But you have to get up and help me *now*."

It took a certain amount of cruelty—not a feature Walter normally had—to force that kid first to sit up, to bear the pain in his head and his jacked up shoulder, then to go through the pain of rising onto his legs.

Matt fell the first time they tried it. Falling meant his shoulder joint bounced and grinded out of its socket, and his head jerked on the landing. His leg wasn't helped by it, either.

But this was no time to be coddling or sympathetic. Not with the last of the light disappearing.

"Get up," Walter told him, making himself sound cold and impatient. "Come on. Hurry up. Let's go."

He wondered if Matt would just pass out again. The pain must have been beyond anything the kid had ever felt.

"Let's go," Walter said, hefting Matt's good arm. Sweat sheeted down the kid's face. But he let Walter guide him back up, one awful movement at a time, until Matt stood balanced on the slope on his shaky good leg.

The key was not to fall. And to do that, they would have to go slow. But they also needed to move forward all the time. If they rested, if Matt fell again, they'd be climbing down this slope in full dark.

It took a good long twenty or thirty minutes for Walter to half-carry the kid to the trail. Once they were there, on relatively flat terrain, Walter let Matt lean back against the rocky hillside to recover.

But he had to do it upright. There would be no more sitting until they made it to the Jeep.

It was too hard to raise him to his feet again. Too hard to get the whole thing moving.

The dislocated shoulder was on Matt's right side, same side as the broken leg. It would have been so much better if Walter could have slung that arm over his shoulder and help the kid walk, but there was no point in wishing what wasn't so.

So Walter positioned himself again on Matt's left side and Matt wrapped his left arm around Walter's shoulder.

It was dark now. Dark and cold.

But Walter knew this trail.

He had pocketed the snacks from Matt's pack, then left the pack behind. Matt couldn't carry it himself anymore, and Walter had his own.

But just a few awkward, difficult steps down the

hill, trying to keep Matt upright while feeling the metal detector hitting him in the back of the skull, and Walter knew he had to ditch his own pack, too. He could come back for it later.

Not the gold, though. That, he would keep with him.

So he struggled to keep the kid upright, while also shucking off his pack, digging inside it for the bag of gold, trying to fit it into his pocket, then realizing he'd better just shove it down the front of his pants.

"What … is that?" Matt managed to ask, panting out the words. The maneuver had taken considerable time.

"Don't worry about it," Walter said. Then he went back to half-carrying the kid down the hill.

Now, as they continued making their slow, excruciating way forward down the dark trail, Walter could feel Matt shaking.

"You all right?" Walter asked him. Stupid question. Of course he wasn't all right.

But Matt took another step forward, and another, and even though the pain must have been terrible, the only sound he made was the whoofs of breath with each footfall, like a train chugging its way up a hill.

"How's your head?" Walter asked him. "Can you see all right?"

Not that there was anything to see but the blackness of a cloudy night.

But the clouds gave off a slight glow, maybe

reflecting a bit of moon, so it wasn't as absolute dark as it could have been.

Normally Walter could have done this hike in an hour.

But moving like this, one slow, painful inch at a time, it would take them double that long, maybe triple.

At least they were moving now. That was something.

The bag of gold was uncomfortable where it was. The pieces were hard and had lots of sharp edges.

Walter had to pause for a moment and reach down and try to shift it.

"Hold on," he told Matt. He needed to do it another way.

He pulled the bag out and dug out handfuls at a time to distribute between his pockets.

Matt panted and waited and sweated. Flecks of sweat came off his face and dripped onto Walter's.

"What is that?" Matt asked again.

"Just some rocks," Walter answered. "It's nothing."

Satisfied now with the more comfortable distribution, Walter braced his arm around Matt's waist and continued to urge him forward.

In time Walter regretted leaving both their waters behind. They were both sweating out the last of their liquid. He hadn't even thought to take a long drink before they set out. The best he could do was try to harvest some off the aspen leaves that they passed. He showed Matt how to do the same.

"I have water in my car," Matt said. He sounded exhausted. He was leaning against Walter more and more.

A six-foot Titan wasn't easy to hold upright. Walter was feeling the exhaustion himself.

They were maybe halfway. It had already taken them an hour and a half.

The night was already as dark as it was going to get. It wasn't raining right now, either.

"Maybe we should take a rest," Walter said.

"Thank God," Matt answered.

Walter led him over to a boulder at the side of the trail where Matt could lean without fully sitting down.

"Here, run your hand up that," Walter said, holding Matt's hand over a clump of tall grass beside him. The blades of it were still saturated from the rain and gave off enough water to lick off his palm and at least wet his tongue.

Walter could do better than that. There were dips in the trail that collected enough rainwater that Walter could scoop it out with his hands, without stirring up too much mud.

He tried carrying a handful of it to Matt, but by the time he reached him, most of it had slipped away.

Then Walter remembered the plastic bag where he'd previously carried his gold.

He gave it a quick rinse in the rainwater, then filled it as full as he could.

It wasn't perfectly water tight, but it did the job well enough. Matt drank several bagfuls in a row.

"It tastes … metal," Matt said.

"Yeah," Walter said. He remembered lying and saying they were rocks. He didn't feel the need to correct that.

"Let's keep going," he said. "Come on, now." He hoisted Matt back up to standing.

"How much farther?" Matt asked.

"Not far," Walter lied.

He could feel Matt's arm shaking again, wrapped around Walter's shoulders.

He wasn't a cruel man. He hated cruelty of any kind. But this effort to get to the Jeep was a necessary punishment. The pain was horrible, he knew, he could imagine it. He could feel how it sapped the strength of this strong young man.

Despite the splint Walter had made, the leg sometimes buckled. Then Walter had to bear all the weight until Matt could stand again.

Even though Matt was alert and awake and talking, his head wound was real. His head must feel like it was being pounded with a hammer.

And that shoulder. Every movement, every jostle must send jolts of pain right through his whole torso.

But the kid was a tough one. He kept inching his

way forward down the trail, sweating and panting and holding himself together.

Walter's body ached from trying to hold up this massive piece of granite. But Walter was a tough one, too, even old as he was, in his mid-fifties, sometimes the oldest guy on a jobsite, with all the kids in their twenties and thirties amazed he could still do the work.

But it wouldn't last forever. Walter couldn't last forever. In the mornings he was a stooped old man stumbling around his rented two-room house, waiting for the pain and stiffness that settled on his bones overnight to gradually ease away.

He had no savings. Who in his group ever did? And he was still a decade away from collecting Social Security.

No wife, no kids, no rich uncle. Who was going to take care of him? No one.

So he kept working construction Monday through Friday, and on the weekends … this.

Bringing his metal detector out to certain spots in these mountains where he knew a certain kind of treasure could be found.

This kid got lucky today. Walter had planned on going to one of his other locations, but at the last minute he changed his mind.

And here, Walter had thought he was the lucky one, since the haul was especially good.

Lucky. Finding this big hulking kid he was presently practically carrying down the mountain.

And then without a sound or a word of warning, Matt collapsed, unconscious, and fell against Walter.

It took him by surprise. He couldn't hold the boy up. Walter fell to the ground along with him.

The splint was an insubstantial, rickety thing after all. The leg looked loose again beneath the knee.

Walter cursed. Tears sprang to his eyes. They had come so far. They were so close. But it was over.

He felt for the pulse at the side of Matt's neck. Still there. And the kid was still breathing.

Maybe it was his head again. Or the pain in his whole body got to be too much. Whatever it was, Walter doubted he would get the boy on his feet to hobble the rest of the way.

It was cold out, but it wasn't raining.

Maybe he could leave him, just for a short while.

Walter knew this stretch of the trail, even in the dark. He had hiked it a hundred times.

Hiked it, but never run it.

He was an old man, feeling older by the minute, but the Jeep wasn't so far away now. And there was help inside it.

An inflatable pad Walter sometimes used during his lunch breaks to lie out and stretch his back if it was particularly stiff.

There were also tie-downs in there, in case he

needed to secure a load on top of the Jeep. And a tow rope and other emergency road gear.

The items arrayed in his mind as Walter took off toward the Jeep. Not at a run, but not a walk, either.

He could make things. He could build things. It was his work for nearly all of his life. Walter's knees and back and shoulders and neck wanted him to slow down, stop rushing down this cobby trail, but Walter's mind said hurry, hurry, keep going. He had an idea now, and it was good.

There was a newest-model Jeep parked near his old one. He couldn't tell the color of it in the dark. It had a canvas top and looked like the kind he would buy for himself if he suddenly had plenty of money.

Walter hadn't thought to get the kid's keys off him. There might be things in there that could help him, too.

But he didn't bother regretting what he didn't have or do. He went about his plan, and gathered what he knew he could use.

He had to slow down some on the way back. It was uphill, the trail was rocky and uneven, and he was tired. More tired than he ever remembered.

And his arms were full. He slung what he could over his shoulders, but the rest he had to carry in his hands.

Matt still lay where Walter left him. Still breathing. Heart still beating.

Maybe it was best that he couldn't feel this. Walter was about to have to hurt him again.

He inflated the pad. Then he made it into a kind of raft. He rigged straps across the length and the width, then threaded the tow rope through them so he could drag Matt on top of the pad down the rest of the trail.

He knew the inflation wouldn't last. The pad would puncture on the sharp rocks. But it would still slide, and that was all he needed.

Well, that, and a team of mules to pull it.

Walter was one of those wiry old men, tanned by years of working outdoors, arms tight with strong, stringy muscles honed by decades of hard labor.

He was the only beast of burden at hand tonight. That would have to do.

With the pad rigged, he laid it right up against Matt's long body, then rolled the kid onto his side. Walter slipped the pad underneath him, and rolled Matt on top.

He had saved a few more straps, and he secured them now, like the little people tying down Gulliver.

Then Walter picked up the tow rope and put his back into it, and started hauling this giant down the trail.

And it nearly broke his back to do it. The pad deflated quickly, and the flattened surface didn't slide as well as Walter hoped.

But there was nothing else to do but keep pulling and hauling until the Jeeps finally came into view.

The newer Jeep might be better, but Walter realized the keys might be in the kid's pack that he left behind. A quick feel of Matt's pockets proved otherwise. Walter used the remote to unlock the doors.

The interior was about the same size as Walter's Jeep, but newer and nicer and cleaner.

More important, the underside of the vehicle looked an inch or two taller than Walter's. That might matter for the water crossing below.

Oh hell, why was he lying? Even if no one was listening but him?

He wanted to drive the better Jeep. So do it. He didn't have to persuade anyone but himself.

It was a trial and a half to figure out how to lift Matt's limp and heavy body into the back of the Jeep. But in the end Walter treated him like cargo, and hauled him hand over hand by the tow rope until the kid rested awkwardly across the available space.

The Jeep started up with a purr. Not with a sound like Walter's as if someone was hand cranking it.

It felt like it must be midnight, but the clock on the dash said it was only close to ten.

The interior smelled new. Leather seats and fresh plastic. Now he'd see how it handled the tricky road.

Even when it was dry, the terrain could jar the

bones right out of your body from all the ruts and rocks along the way.

But a good rain made the holes that much deeper. Matt moaned when they hit another rock.

"Stay down," Walter told him as he maneuvered around another deep and bone-jarring hole. There was nothing good in the boy waking up now.

Walter couldn't help smiling to himself and then quietly, privately whooping. He had done the impossible. They had gotten this far.

He didn't agree with men who couldn't take pride in their work. There were small enough victories in life. You had to enjoy them when you could.

In the headlights he could see the stream crossing up ahead. He brought the Jeep to a stop and studied it. He was right, the water looked deeper than it was this afternoon. The question was how deep. Too deep to get through?

But what choice did he have? They had come this far, he couldn't stop now. He had to get this poor kid to the hospital. What else could they do, just sit here and wait?

Walter whispered a plea and he drove ahead.

He could hear the water lapping against the sides of the Jeep, much higher than he liked to hear.

But the vehicle kept going, it didn't swamp out, it didn't stall, it didn't float.

Then more rutted, rocky road ahead, but the worst was behind them. At least Walter hoped so.

The last part of the road had obviously slid. Mud carpeted it down toward the asphalt.

But the paved road looked clear, as far as Walter could see. He would keep driving until something made him stop.

There were boulders in the road here and then, from where they had tumbled down muddy slopes in the sleet and rain.

But there was no other traffic out, so Walter drove in whatever lane he needed to carefully pick his way through.

He knew exactly where cell service kicked in again, twelve miles down this road. Even then, he couldn't help looking at his phone, waiting for the full fat bars to show up again at the top.

At twelve miles, right on schedule, his phone allowed him to make the call.

The closest hospital was another fifty-five miles away. There were clinics in town, but nothing that could handle what Walter was bringing them.

It would take a helicopter, and dispatch got on it right away. Told Walter where to drive to meet them.

He drove carefully—no sense in being reckless now, when he was so close—all the rest of the way down into town.

Then a little ways further, to where the helicopter was.

To where a team was ready to take over.

"Name's Matt," Walter told them. "That's all I know." He gave them a brief rundown of the boy's injuries.

But they were professionals and knew how to find out more. They had his wallet and Jeep registration in less than a minute.

"His folks called it in," one of the paramedics said. "Glad you found him. I'm sure they'll want to thank you."

Walter waved that away. "No need. Although … I need to know where to return the kid's Jeep. Why don't you write down the address. I'll find them myself."

That was as much conversation as they had time for. Matt had already been loaded onto a proper backboard that was now being loaded into the chopper.

Walter waited outside and watched it take off. Then he stiffly climbed back into the Jeep.

He sat there for a while, not starting the car, just staring out into the night.

It wouldn't do to just get up and go again. A night like this was worthy of some thought.

Walter's whole body felt pained and overused. Worse than the hardest day out on a site.

But he felt an intense satisfaction deep in his gut. He had done something. He had really done it.

There weren't a lot of times in a man's life when he could look at himself and say good, what you did was good.

But Walter knew he had done good for that boy. He had seen it all the way through.

He also knew there was a strange bit of luck at work. Putting him there, where he was, just in time.

Ten minutes earlier or later, he wouldn't have heard the kid cry out. He had to be there right where he was, when he was.

He wouldn't have accidentally stumbled on the boy, Matt was too far up the hill. Walter would have passed by him and never known.

And Walter wouldn't have been there at all on that mountain today if not for his secret hobby. He had to factor that in, too—maybe more than all the rest.

There was a secret Walter kept from all his friends and his co-workers. Something he knew others might think too shameful for anyone to do.

But maybe none of them had been as poor as he had been for so long. Poor since he was a little boy.

Sometimes you learn a skill and it stays with you, even if no one else would want to do it.

His Uncle Jack, an old carpenter who grew up in Montana, visited Walter and his father when Walter was small.

Uncle Jack was poor, too, as poor as Walter and his dad. But he had a way of finding extra cash.

"There are places up in the mountains," he said, "the pretty lookouts where people can drive to. A lot of people take their loved ones' ashes up there, and dump them over the rail."

But the mountains aren't like the ocean, he said, and the ashes don't just disappear like they would in water.

They fall down below, on the rocks and ledges.

And if you take the time to study it, you can find out where.

"The morticians don't sift out the gold teeth, see," Uncle Jack said. "The gold melts, but it's still in the ash."

Uncle Jack made a weekend hobby out of taking his metal detector up into the mountains to find the gold crowns from among the tossed out ash.

The price of gold shifts up and down over time, Uncle Jack said, but sometimes a month's worth of gold teeth might be enough to make your rent.

Walter's father had said it was gruesome. No better than stealing from the dead.

But Uncle Jack had winked at little Walter. "You see the sense in it, don't you, boy?"

Sometimes there were gold rings, too, which always surprised Walter. He assumed the families would ask for any jewelry to be removed.

But no one would ever think about their loved ones' teeth. Except Walter, who depended on them to live.

Soon he wouldn't be able to work anymore. His broken down body was especially broken down tonight.

But he could still hike his few special trails well into old age, climb down the relevant slopes, hunt for his gold.

But maybe, Walter thought, there was something else here at work. The strange way the universe got its own way.

Who's to say his Uncle Jack didn't plant that seed fifty years ago, just so Walter could save young Matt on that mountain tonight? Maybe the boy was going to grow up to be somebody. President, or an important scientist or inventor.

Maybe Matt would be the one to look back on tonight and say there was a reason that old man Walter was there.

It was only because of that old man that I became what I am today…

Whatever that would be. Maybe Walter would never know.

But it made a man wonder, all the various twists and turns. Why this, why that, why him.

Walter started up the Jeep, the fancy new one. He

would drive it home tonight and find a way to get his own Jeep back tomorrow. He also had to retrieve his pack and the boy's. A few details to be tidied up.

That included contacting the boy's parents to return the Jeep. Maybe if they offered him some reward for saving their son, he wouldn't say no.

He hadn't done it for the money—that never entered his mind. He did it because a decent man would never do otherwise.

Besides, the afternoon had already brought a good haul. Probably the best he'd had in a long time.

Walter pulled out one of the kid's snack bars he still kept wedged along with the gold inside his right pocket. There was a frozen dinner waiting for him at home, but there was no reason to wait to feed himself then.

He rolled down the window and crooked his arm on the ledge. The air still felt moist, but it smelled fresh. Not dangerous anymore, but clean.

The clouds had broken up, too, so a few stars were sparkling through.

It had been a good day. A hard one, a rough one, but a good one after all.

Despite all the pain in Walter's body, he wouldn't have it any other way.

"Rescue me?" the boy had asked, quirking up the sides of his mouth.

Damn straight, Walter should have told him. That's why the road led me here. Now buck up and let's get going. I've got a kid to save tonight.

***

TAKEN AT RUSTLER PASS

TAKEN AT RUSTLER PASS

In Alpine Ridge we love each other. Whether you're a busboy or the school principal or the pharmacist at Walmart, we know you, we know your family, we care about you. Or at least we pay attention to whatever you're doing. Sound carries here. Last week the Claussens had a fight and someone heard little Raina Claussen shouting, "Mom! Don't!" and every one knew about it by morning. Because we care.

So it's hard to be new. People notice you.

But somehow he slipped by.

Someone would have called Sheriff Burns. They would have shunned Black Coat Man so fast he would have realized by day two this wasn't going to work. People would see and know.

But he was good. If you can ever say evil is good.

The railing of the bridge was slick and cold. I didn't want to touch it. I didn't want to be here at all. I had been crying for the last two hours.

Rain and wind had spent the day ripping all the pretty yellow leaves off the aspens. It would all start to look dead soon. That included me.

He stood behind me, too close, so cozy and warm in his long wool coat. I could smell the wet wool and that made me cry, too. I used to love that smell, it reminded me of my grandfather. He smoked a pipe and I loved that smell, too. This man behind me was a monster. I wanted to kill him. I already tried.

It was close to dark now. That was what he wanted. We'd been holed up in his windowless van so long I was sure I would never see light again. He didn't do what you think. That's not what this was about. Some people have desires that have nothing to do with that.

I shivered and I'm sure he liked that. I was wearing jogging shorts and a short-sleeved shirt. I thought about that, how someone would have to guess what I'd been wearing last. Would my mother know it was the lime green shorts? The neon pink running top, so I could be visible on the road? She would remember the pale pink hoodie, but that was gone. He took it.

I had gone out for a run while the weather was still mild. Around eleven o'clock in the morning. It was Saturday and all I had to do was homework and clean my room. Sundays were the big cleaning days.

I had my cell phone, I wasn't stupid. I ran on the left side of the road, facing traffic. All the regular safety precautions, but like I said, it wasn't really necessary because people look out for each other. My right arm was usually tired from waving every time a car went by, like one of those mechanical Lucky Cats you see in Chinese restaurants. Wave, smile, wave, smile.

Not that I ever minded. It's nice to see drivers slow down, sometimes roll down their windows. "Hey, Megan!" "Look at you go!" Some kind of encouragement. They all know I run cross-country at our high school—I win a lot of races. People are used to seeing me on my long training runs up the dirt road just outside our village.

Black Coat Man must have been watching me to know. For how long? A few days, seeing me run after school? Or maybe a whole week? Did he see me out here last Saturday and know he would have plenty of chances to catch me along my route?

Or was it just random? Thought he'd drive out the road toward Rustler Pass this morning, see what he could find. Look! Here's one. Drive on and get ready.

Normally there isn't a lot of traffic on Rustler Pass. It's just a two-lane dirt road with some pretty steep drop-offs down toward the river on one side, and no guard rails.

You'd take it to go hiking somewhere or mountain biking. But with the road construction on Highway 50, a lot of the locals have been going this way during the week to get to their jobs in Carbon Creek and some of the bigger towns. On the weekends, it's mostly just sporty locals and tourists.

I came around the bend on one of the stretches of road where it's high solid rock on one side, and a cliff dropping to the river on the other.

There are lots of pullouts so the slower drivers can do the right thing and get out of the way of someone more confident on the road. Or out of the way of vacation campers and dirt trucks or anything else taking up more than half the space.

He was at one of the pullouts. I could see him in the distance, an old roly-poly man, bald, thick-looking glasses, long wrinkled khaki pants and a button down flannel shirt, looking like half the tourists who come here in autumn to gawk at the beautiful leaves.

I did all the things they say you shouldn't do. I fell for it.

Man with a van? Check. Asks for help? Check. *"My heart! Can you help me get my pills?"* You go to the passenger side, where he's pointing, and where no one passing on the road might see what was about to happen. Check.

But he was old and he didn't look like any kind of threat. Dumb.

I felt a sharp stab in my leg, and that was the last

thing I knew before waking up tied up in the back of the dark van.

What do you do? You scream. You thrash around. You kick. You cry. You wear yourself out, this can't be happening, dear God, this isn't true—and he watched the whole thing, laughing. Chuckling. So delighted with me and with himself.

He'd gotten a live one.

Like a fisherman so thrilled to have to fight that big tarpon on his line. The longer it takes, the better. The more worth it.

I finally got that.

And by then I was exhausted. I hadn't eaten in hours. I'd already run for miles. And now I was terrified and sad and so angry. It took everything out of me, for a while.

He hummed a lot. Tunes I didn't know. It didn't matter, he just wanted to show me how happy he was. How in charge.

He called me girly.

"Girly, did you know when you woke up it was gonna be your last day?"

"Girly, you think your momma's gonna miss you soon?"

"Girly…"

I shut him out, as best I could. I had to think. *Think.*

Inside the van, I had no idea where we were. That van was my whole world for a while. The smell of it—

sweat and bad breath and stale food. Dirty socks and underwear. Black Coat Man wasn't tidy. He wasn't clean.

He'd tricked it out with a whole living space: narrow bed, hot plate, fold-out table, the works.

I was scrunched up on the floor, between the bed and the table, my arms tied behind me, killing me.

"Not much longer now, girly."

Every time he said something like that, it made me start crying again. I couldn't help it. Even though I couldn't stand how much he loved it.

But a part of me, the angry part of me, was still trying to work out what to do. Even as tears flooded down my face.

What did I have? Nothing. Just me. No cell phone—he probably threw that off the cliff down to the river. No weapons. Nothing.

But not nothing. I've been an athlete all my life. Even with my arms strapped behind me, my legs were still free. He had to leave them that way for me to scrunch down where I was, straddling the base of the table.

My legs, long and strong.

I waited for my chance.

I whimpered. "The rope is hurting me. Please. Just a little looser. I swear I won't do anything."

I think it was adding that last part that made him suspicious.

But he fell for it, a little, and did come just a bit closer. Maybe to see if my wrists were bleeding—he would have liked that.

I waited and I timed it. Just as his head was dipping down, I kicked out my right leg, and I almost caught him square in the temple with my heel.

But he was suspicious, like I said, and he moved fast for an old man. He caught my leg at the ankle.

"I can chop it!" he shouted. "I will!"

He opened a box on top of the table and took out a long knife.

"You want me to? Huh?" His eyes were big and wild. I could see the whites of them all around his pupils, lit up even in the dark van.

I thought he might do it. So I cried and begged. He was crazy. I didn't want him to cut me.

It took him a while to settle down. He breathed really hard for at least fifteen or twenty minutes, mumbling to himself, finally humming again.

"No, I have something better," he told me. "Much better."

I didn't want to know what it was.

There was a rifle racked on the wall above the bed. A deer rifle. Maybe he knew how to shoot it, maybe he didn't. Maybe it was just for show, like his red flannel shirt. Part of pretending to be a tourist. Or a hunter. Who knows.

I knew how to shoot, but it didn't matter. Not with

my arms tied behind me. Not unless I got free somehow.

That was all I did, minute by minute: make plans. Have ideas. Think, Megan, *think*. I didn't know why he was waiting so long, but it gave me time. Time to drive myself out of my mind with one scheme after another.

After a while I could hear rain pounding the roof. This time of year, October, it might rain, it might snow. It was cold inside the van, but I still had my pink hoodie then. He didn't cut it off until he made me go outside.

"Please, Mister," I said at some point. He liked me calling him *mister*. I could see that. "I'm just a kid."

"I'm just a kid," he whined, mocking me. Then he laughed at me for even trying. I clamped my teeth together and didn't talk again.

Finally it was dark enough for his purpose. Just the cusp of dusk. The rain had stopped and the sky was still covered in gray clouds. They were tinged in red and purple now, at sunset. Pretty, if I wasn't where I was. If I was home safe, looking out our living room window, smelling my mom's dinner cooking, hearing my brother and my dad talking about whatever—all of it. So precious. I could barely keep it together, thinking about it.

How I was going to miss them. How much they were going to miss me. How horrible it would be for my parents, finding my body somewhere…

"Let's go," he said, grabbing me roughly by my left arm. The ropes bit into my wrists. I didn't whimper, didn't say a word. He didn't deserve any sounds from me anymore.

It was hard for me to get up. My body was crammed into that awkward space, and my legs were stiff by now. But he was suddenly in a hurry. He had waited, and waited, and now it was time. Right *now*.

When he finally got me outside the van, I looked around us immediately, frantically, trying to figure out where we were.

The van was parked at the end of a different dirt road. All around us was forest. Huge shapes of fir trees and aspens and spruce. Everything still wet from the rain. The ground beneath me muddy.

But it wasn't the trees that interested me. I love the trees, I'm used to them.

It was the bridge up ahead, shiny with raindrops glistening on the metal railing.

That's where he started dragging me to.

I had to fight not to scream.

Because suddenly I knew. I understood. I knew where we were.

I had hiked up here before with my parents and my brother. All of us, out for a Sunday hike with our old yellow Lab, Klondike.

The hiking trail ended right here where it intersected with the old mining road. Beyond was the old mine itself, shut down for decades now, but still dangerous. Incredibly dangerous.

The mining company had finally agreed to install a big metal door over the entrance to the mine after the fourth kid in four years fell down a shaft, exploring. Four dead kids will finally get someone's attention.

There was still old equipment lying around, rusting. There was still a pit filled with dirty, rusty water, and a stream ran from it that we had to keep shouting at Klondike to get away from. Who knows what was in that reddish brown water. It probably would have killed him.

We finally had to leash him up and hike back instead of just yelling at the poor dog. He didn't know, he was tired and thirsty.

I wasn't sorry to leave it. The place was eerie and dirty and depressing.

Not at all like the rest of the pretty forest all around it, with glacier lilies and columbine growing in the shade of the trees.

Further on, further than we were willing to explore while we had the dog, there was a bridge that went from the entrance of the mine out across the pit. There was a building on the other side of it, maybe the mine office or something. The bridge wasn't very long, but it was high up. The pit went down a long way below it.

That's where Black Coat Man was dragging me. Pulling me along by my aching arm. I didn't go easily.

You wouldn't. You wouldn't just give up and let him take you. Not after thinking so hard for the past however many hours, making plans, having so many ideas.

I dug in my feet. I fought him. I fought him until he made the first cut.

It was down my cheek, a cut with a knife I didn't even see him holding. A smaller one, much shorter than the one he threatened me with in the van. Compact, easy to carry in one hand while he was hauling me along with the other.

"I can cut you all day, girly," he said, breathing hard again now. I could smell the blood dripping down my sliced cheek. I could smell his sour, excited breath.

The cut hurt so bad, but I pressed my mouth closed. I wouldn't scream. I wouldn't cry. He wanted that too much.

"You want more?!" he shouted. He wasn't afraid of anyone hearing us. Up here, at the end of the abandoned road, no one would ever hear us.

I kept digging in my feet. I still had my running shoes on, with good tread for the dirt surface.

He used the knife again, and he cut off my hoodie in strips: first the back of it, then the front, then the sleeves. Once he'd shredded it enough, he ripped it off me. It was cold out. Too cold. No matter how I tried not to, I started to shiver.

"Not long now, girly," he said, and he was humming again, like what he said was the lyric of a song.

He was old, but he was still strong enough to pull me along. And he had the knife, and I was all too aware of it in his other hand, and I could feel the blood dripping from the stinging cut in my cheek onto my bright pink shirt.

Despair takes over. I won't lie. As strong as I was trying to be, it finally got to me. That I was going to die soon. That this was it. There was no one coming to help me. I probably wasn't getting away.

Probably, I still told myself. A shred of hope. Maybe not, probably not, but … maybe.

It took him longer than he must have planned for with me resisting, because by the time we were finally standing on that bridge, looking down at the dark dirty water below, dusk was already almost over, and night was almost here.

He was in a hurry again. Or still. Because it was no good if he couldn't see.

That was the whole point, to see it. To see me. To take some random girl from the road, bring her up here, make her jump. Or push her. I wasn't sure how he was going to do it. But he wanted to make me die, and he wanted to watch it. That was the thrill. That was his plan.

Then he surprised me. He cut the ropes around my wrists.

Maybe he thought it would look like an accident or suicide that way, although how anyone would explain the cut to my cheek or the welts all over my wrists, I didn't know.

Then he surprised me again, and sliced his sharp knife down my bare right arm.

I couldn't help it, I cried out. I slapped my left hand over the wound, trying to stop the blood, trying to stop the pain.

He pressed the knife against my cheek. "Don't you try anything, girly." He had that crazed white-eyed look again. "I'll cut you all over. I'll skin you alive."

He jammed the knife against my ribs. He gripped my left arm hard. I tried to think how I could get away. Twist? Knock the knife out of his hand? But even with my mind racing, the reality was too hard. He had me too tight. The knife was right there. He would stab me, I knew it. Cut me again. He didn't care. He could do this all night.

And then it came.

The sound.

Blaring through the trees.

It's hard to understand an elk call if you've never heard it before. It goes on way longer than you expect. It sounds like a mixture of a scream, a fire alarm, and the wailing of a ghost.

You don't know which direction it's coming from. It echoes, it vibrates, and the scream goes on and on.

And if you're from the city, and you've never heard it before, it's frightening. It's jarring. It's unreal.

But I knew what it was. I've lived here all my life. I know elk, I know deer.

I know salvation when I hear it.

Once, when Klondike was a younger dog and we still had to keep the shock collar on him to keep him from chasing wildlife, my dad and I were out hiking in the mountains above the village, when suddenly Klondike flushed a little speckled fawn.

They depend on camouflage right up until the last minute. So that fawn had been hunkered down beneath a little bush, right off the side of the trail, just a few steps away, and I never saw it. You wouldn't. But Klondike nosed around and could smell it.

People think of deer as silent, but they're not. They scream, too.

It all happened so fast. The little fawn screamed, loud like someone leaning on their horn, and it popped up and took off so quickly, Klondike barely had time to react.

The fawn was already halfway to the safety of the trees before Klondike started to chase it.

By then my dad was punching the button on his transmitter for the shock collar, giving Klondike a few sharp shocks, and he was shouting at him, "NO!" and meanwhile the fawn was getting away.

And then the mama deer got involved. She was in

the trees, where the baby was running now, and I never saw her before that, either. They both must have heard my dad and Klondike and me coming, and the mama sneaked into the forest, but the baby was born with instinct. It knew it was too slow to get away, so it counted on its camouflage and hunkered down beneath that little bush.

But now the mama was *activated*. She gave a cry, too, a short bellow of outrage and alarm, and she started running in wide circles around us, once, twice, maybe four or five times. Trying to draw us away. No, come after *me*, she was saying. Running around us, watching us, warning us.

It was scary. I thought she might attack us. Deer do, sometimes. There are videos of it, deer attacking hunters. So we kept hiking fast, and my dad kept his finger on the transmitter button in case Klondike needed more reminding, and we got out of there as fast as we could.

I was so grateful Klondike never hurt that fawn. I never would have been able to get over it.

But now I thought about it. About all of that. The whole scene whipped through my mind in a fraction of the time it takes to tell it.

It came to me because that strategy worked. The scream, the bolt, the dash for the trees.

But you have to do it *now*. No hesitation. You have to GO.

The elk's scream had broken Black Coat Man's concentration. It had spooked him. Confused him. Just for a moment.

His grip on me slackened. The knife jerked away from my side.

That quick moment was all I needed. If I did it now. If I went.

If I ran.

I was the fawn. I bolted away right then. I didn't look back. I didn't wait. I didn't worry.

I ran fast, like I can, like I always have. I ran off the bridge. Across the dirt. Blood flying off my cheek and my freshly-sliced arm. My shoes digging into the fresh mud, then angling upward, off the old mining road, into the trees.

He was shouting at me. Screaming at me. I could hear his feet on the metal bridge as he tried to come after me.

He was still shouting and his voice was closer, like he'd made it to the road and closer to the van, but I was already in the trees, stumbling over roots and logs in the dark, and I knew he had a rifle in that van, but it didn't matter.

He would never find me. Never get me. It was dark and he would never follow me into the woods.

But he kept screaming at me, shouting, and it let me know I was getting further and further away.

There was a quality to the air now. A familiar heaviness I knew.

I could smell it: the iron smell of my blood, the heavy metallic smell of the air. Like a sheet of steel about to squeeze down on me and encase me.

It wasn't rain that was coming soon, it was snow.

I was wearing just my jogging shorts and shirt.

This wouldn't be good. I had to keep running.

I thought I could hear the sound of a motor somewhere behind me. He must have started up the van. He would drive the road. He would look for me. I had to stay deep in the trees.

It was probably an hour, hour and a half's run from here back to Alpine Ridge. And that was in daylight and good weather—and on the road.

At night, running overland through a thick forest, dodging fallen limbs and logs and tangles of undergrowth I wouldn't be able to see, it might take me twice that long. At least.

And to do it at night, overland, in the *snow*. Wearing just shorts and a flimsy shirt.

It … didn't look good.

My mind was still racing, right along with my feet. I tripped over something, sprawled.

I banged my knees hard doing that. Cut my palms where they flew out to brace me.

But I was on my feet again, tears streaming down

my face, ignoring all the pain, just running. Only running.

But it showed me what I already knew. Back in my thinking mind.

The snow was coming down now, wet and cold, burning the cuts on my cheek and arm. It made the ground slick. And if it kept up like this, the snow would start piling up, and that would slow me down even more.

My feet just wanted to keep running, they just wanted me to get away, but the thinking part of me understood.

There was really only one way to get out of here, if I was smart about it. I had to run on the road. Even though it was a terrible risk. Black Coat Man might be driving right where I was, searching for me, and next thing I knew, I'd be right back where I was.

Or worse.

But what was worse than dying, no matter how it happened? Being pushed over a bridge, freezing to death—I didn't want any of it.

So I had to take the chance.

My body was starting to shiver again. Even slowing down a little, in the falling wet snow, made everything feel much colder. My sweaty clothes were starting to freeze.

I angled downward, aiming sideways along the

slope, carefully picking my way down so I wouldn't fall and tumble all the way to the bottom.

I didn't see headlights. I didn't hear a motor. As soon as I reached the old mining road again I could pick up the pace.

Where was he? He wouldn't give up. I was a witness. I was still alive. He didn't know if maybe I memorized his license plate—I didn't, I never saw it—or if I would be able to lead law enforcement right to him.

He must have been panicked, too. Afraid of what this random girl might do to him, if he let her get away.

When I was close to the road, a few feet above it, still hidden in trees, I waited and listened hard. But still, nothing. No sound of a motor.

So I took the chance. I hopped down the rest of the way, and then I ran faster, free to pour on the speed now that I didn't have to worry about anything underfoot.

I was always looking ahead, behind, ready to bolt back up the slope if I saw the headlights or heard an engine. But he wasn't there. The van wasn't there. I ran and ran as fast as I could.

The snow was heavier all the time, falling so freely it made me sick. Why now? Couldn't it wait? Where was the help from above when I needed it?

I slid around a curve in the road, too fast, and

almost ran off the trail, and it was there, right there, he was waiting. Not running the motor or using the headlights, but holding a big bright flashlight that was cutting through the darkness and the snow, and it caught me, square in its light.

I gave a yelp of fear, I couldn't help it, and I dashed up the slope to my left.

He shouted out, "Girly! I got you! Come on down!"

As if I would.

My whole body was shaking. From adrenaline, from cold, from fear.

I wrapped my arms around my torso, but it did nothing to make me warm.

I was breathing hard now, my mind was racing. I could go back up through the trees. I would. I just needed to catch my breath. I just needed to catch up with my overloaded heart.

He was coming toward where I hid. I could see the beam of his big light. He was laughing. "Come out, come out! I got you!" Like it was a game. Like this wasn't real.

He shot a round into the trees, close enough to me that he might have gotten lucky. The deer rifle had enough range. But he still couldn't see me in the dark to know exactly where to shoot.

"Come out, come out! Girly!" Then the sing-song sound of his voice changed. "COME OUT!" He shot the rifle again. Way off to my left. He was just guessing.

I had my wits back. The sound of the gun cleared them. He was crazy. He wasn't going to stop. He was going to kill me if he could.

I knew that. I already knew that. But something inside me clicked.

I wasn't helpless. I could do things, too.

I just hadn't decided yet until now.

You get into a pattern, all your life. Of trying to be kind. Of trying to be fair.

It's why it hurts so much and shocks you when someone else doesn't play by those rules.

It's why begging would never work. It's why I would never be able to convince him. This wasn't *logic*, this wasn't normal, this was evil.

Only evil.

It was hard to move quietly with my limbs shaking from the cold, but the snow was muffling sound anyway. It was helping me after all.

I did what that mother deer did, taking a wide circle around him, not close enough that he could hurt me, but still close enough to keep watch.

He was still shining his big light off where I was before. He had no idea I had moved.

When I was far enough away, in the direction where he wasn't looking, I crossed the road. There were woods on the other side, too. This wasn't Rustler Pass, where there was a steep drop-off to one side. The old mining road ran straight through the forest.

I was still shaking, but I wasn't crying anymore. I could feel the pain from the places where he cut me, the pain in my knees and palms from when I fell, but the cold snow was soothing, in its way. Like icing a sore muscle.

I would need to get warm soon. I couldn't go on like this. No matter what else was happening, the cold and the snow were real. They would kill me soon if I didn't change things.

"GIRLY!" Impatient again. Maybe afraid. Another round from the deer rifle. Good. The sound was loud and he didn't hear me.

I had picked up a branch, suitable to the task. I've played plenty of softball in my life, and I'm a crack bat.

I swung it hard, I swung it fast, I didn't hesitate, I hit him hard.

The branch cracked the back of his skull. Black Coat Man went down before he ever knew I was there.

I had to move fast. I was freaked out. By myself, by him, by all of it.

I ran to the van, yanked the driver's door open.

The keys weren't there.

I had to run back to him, to touch him, to slap against the pockets of his long wool coat and feel for them. I felt the lump. I dug them out.

My hands were shaking so badly now it's a wonder I could feed the key in the slot. But as soon as I did, the engine started and the heater started with it, and for the first time in all those hours, I felt hope again.

I had to pause for a few minutes to sob. Head leaning against the steering wheel, the fear and desperation flooding through me.

But I couldn't spare more time than that. What if he woke up? What if he came to the door and it suddenly opened and the whole thing started all over?

There was only one way to be sure. It made me sick, but my mind insisted.

The van was pointing away from where he lay in the road. I could see the lump of him in the rearview mirror.

I only hesitated a moment. Then I put the van in reverse.

I felt the thud, the bump, but I didn't care. Not then. It was the only way to be safe.

Then I shifted to Drive, I jammed my foot hard against the pedal, and I drove away from there so fast I almost lost control on another curve and would have gone flying into the trees.

I slowed down. I had to. I had to breathe again.

I rattled down the last stretch of the old mining road, where it was rocky and rough, until it met up with Rustler Pass. I knew this road now. You run in a place and it's part of your skin, your muscles, your bones. I knew, even in the dark, where to be careful, how not to drive off the cliff. But there was no moderation now. No caution. I just wanted speed. I wanted to be home.

At the entrance to Alpine Ridge, I could see flashing lights from three different cars. My parents must have called Sheriff Burns. They were going to search for me. Maybe people already were.

I should have been home from my run just a few hours after I set out. Mama deer was worried. She would have called for help before it was dark.

I leaned on the horn. I leaned on it and shouted. I screamed. Sound carries in Alpine Ridge, even in the falling snow. "I'M HERE! I'M HERE!"

Choking, crying, "I'M HERE!"

I could say this: They didn't go look for him until the next morning, and the snow had covered him by then. He was dead, I was glad of it, and I didn't need to know exactly which of the things killed him.

Was it me cracking the branch against his skull?

Running over him with his own van?

Was he still alive then, but unconscious, and then he died from exposure, lying out all night in the cold?

But that isn't what happened. I won't lie.

They did go look for him. That night. Right where I said he would be.

They could follow the tire tracks that left two deep grooves in the snow. Even though those grooves were quickly getting covered over.

There was blood in the snow. Plenty of it. There was no mystery about where he had fallen.

But he wasn't there. The body wasn't there.

At first I panicked when I heard it. He was alive. He would come for me again. Or he had gotten away, and would do this to somebody else.

I was distraught. It wasn't possible.

Even in my warm, cozy house, safe again, warm from the shower that washed away my blood and restored the heat to my bones, when Sheriff Burns told me that, I screamed. It just came out. I clamped my hand over my mouth, as if someone might hear it and find me.

But that wasn't the end.

Hunters fill the woods this time of year. It isn't safe to hike in the mountains if you're not dressed in bright orange.

Even then, some of the yahoos from out of state end up shooting their buddies every now and then, or accidentally killing someone's dog. They're not professionals, they're just tourists, out to kill some of our deer and elk because everyone knows it's easy to get hunting tags here.

It was about a week before one of those guys came charging into the sheriff's station, all sweaty and pale, the way I heard it, rambling about a body in the woods.

It was naked. It had been picked over by some

predator or scavenger, but of course anyone could still tell it was him.

How he got there is anyone's guess.

But I have a theory.

In Alpine Ridge we love each other. We look out for each other. We do.

Why did that elk scream, allowing me to get away? Why did the snow fall, muffling the sound of me sneaking up on him?

Why was I out there that day, why did he pick me? Me, out of all the other young women or teenage girls who might have been jogging or riding their bikes?

I think there is order in this world. I think there is justice. I think that evil has no place here, and that evil is *seen to.*

I played a part. That elk played a part. The snow, the cold—and maybe some hunter played a part.

Maybe the sheriff or someone searching for me, one of their own, a girl born and raised in Alpine Ridge—maybe somebody thought it was better to take matters into their own hands and drag that body into the woods. To be fed upon, to be found later—who knows? I don't think I will ever know.

Our old dog Klondike flushed a fawn when I was twelve years old. I saw the whole thing play out, and remembered it.

Maybe that was the day. Some force in the world said, "That's her. That's our girl. She can do it."

And four years later it was me that that evil man stole, there on Rustler Pass.

"Girly! Come out! I got you!"

But he didn't. I got him first.

THE OUTPOST AWAY FROM THE WORLD

1

Julia unlocked the door to her mother's cabin. She hesitated at the threshold, surprised by how nervous she suddenly felt.

A few dust motes danced in the air, stirred up by the open door. Afternoon sunlight streamed through the two big windows in the main room, falling on the familiar couch with the denim slipcover, the old wool rug, the Franklin stove, the Douglas fir plank table her father had made as a first anniversary gift, before he decided that Julia's mother, Annika Ross, was too crazy to live with, even though there was already a child on the way.

The dog at Julia's side didn't hesitate at all. Flicka bounded into the room and began her inspection, nosing along the walls, the furniture, checking behind the stove where the mice liked to hide.

The four-year-old black Lab was Julia's dog now, part of her inheritance. Along with this cabin.

The place had been empty for over a year, yet it looked as clean and tidy as if Annika had just swept it and dusted and mopped before Julia arrived.

Her mother had warned her that it would look like this: cared for. Loved. Julia had nodded and pretended to go along, even though her mother knew she didn't believe in any of it anymore.

Satisfied with the front room, Flicka continued on into the two small bedrooms. Julia remained in the doorway, still surveying what had once been her home.

She had spent exactly half of her life here, until she was fourteen. How had the two of them lived here together for so long, in such a tiny, confining space, with only books and chores and conversation to fill their time?

Her mother had had her work, but Julia wasn't part of that.

It was, eventually, what drove Julia from ever wanting to come back here.

But now, seeing it almost a decade and a half later, she felt an unexpected affection for the place. She breathed in the familiar scent of it: the pine and pitch of the wooden walls and floors; the old, cold ash in the Franklin stove; the musty flowers and herbs drying in bundles hanging by string from the ceiling for her mother to use later for cooking or her various tinctures.

Her parents had built this cabin with their own hands. Julia's father was a skilled and meticulous carpenter, and Annika was both a hard worker and an enthusiastic partner. He taught, she learned. Enough that even after he left them, she was able to continue improving the little house over the years.

She added a root cellar and expanded the pantry to accommodate the bounty from her garden. She built a second bedroom so Julia could have her own, then later added a tiny bathroom with a special composting toilet so the two of them wouldn't have to use the outhouse anymore.

When Julia was eight she helped her mother build a wooden shower stall outside at the rear of the cabin. Until then, they bathed in a metal tub. They still had to haul up their water from the stream and heat it by the kettleful on the stove, but now they could pour it into a perforated tub on the roof of the stall and enjoy the luxury of a short but warm shower.

It had all felt like such an adventure when Julia was young. Like *Little House on the Prairie,* transplanted to the mountains. Just her mother and her, living alone out in the woods.

Although according to Julia's mother, they were far from alone.

It was talk like that that eventually drove Julia's father away.

He had imagined a different life with the tall Nordic goddess he had met at the restaurant where they both worked. Annika Ross and Gerardo Rosales had both escaped their families and their city lives in Denver to move the small Colorado ski town of Altar Peak to hide from the noise of the world.

During the winters, when his carpentry work tapered off, Gerardo filled in as a cook at one of the upscale burger grills in town. One day Annika walked in as the new server, and by the end of her first shift, Gerardo was in love.

By the spring, she had convinced him that even the town was too busy to live in. They should go into the mountains. Build a little cabin. Live off the land, just the two of them.

They quickly got married and did just that.

But Annika had left out a few important details.

She was confident she could grow enough food for them in the garden she intended to plant. But she neglected to tell her new husband the methods she intended to use.

Flicka was back now, apparently satisfied with her inspection of the entire house. She jumped onto the denim couch and lay with her chin propped on one of the red cushions, waiting for whatever might come next.

Julia finally stepped all the way inside and shut the door behind her. She crossed to the couch and sank down beside Flicka and stroked the dog's smooth black back.

She closed her eyes and rested. It had already been a long day. Buying supplies in town, making arrangements to be driven to the trailhead, then hiking the six miles here, carrying a heavy pack.

She knew there would probably be plenty of jars of jams and pickled beets and other fruits and vegetables her mother preserved, but beyond that, she had no idea what food might still be here, unspoiled by mice or other creatures.

She brought a small bag of dog food, a loaf of bread, a bag of coffee—she would definitely need coffee—and a few other staples to get her through the week.

Even though her mother hadn't been here to tend the garden this year, Julia noticed on the way in that it was as robust as ever, although definitely wilder and more overgrown. There would be enough there to harvest for a week of salads and other meals.

But tonight, maybe just a peanut butter sandwich with one of her mother's jams would have to do. A bowl of kibble for Flicka. Anything more complicated would require Julia to haul in firewood and get the Franklin stove going again.

She should probably do that anyway. Even in the

summer, the nights could get cold. By midnight, she and the dog would probably appreciate the warmth.

Julia checked her watch. Almost 5:00. Even though sunset wasn't officially until around 8:00, up this high the sun disappeared early behind the the flat-topped Altar Peak that gave the town and the ski resort their names. After that, there would be only a shadowy twilight for a while, followed by the absolute darkness of a night lit only by moon and stars.

Julia would need to gather the candles and the oil lamps. At one point her mother had flirted with lanterns fueled by small cans of propane, but she didn't like the constant hissing sound they made. She preferred the quiet of old-fashioned light.

Annika had talked about maybe adding solar panels to the roof one day, and finally bringing electricity to the cabin. But it was just one more thing on a long list that would have to remain undone.

There was no point in dwelling on any of the others.

Julia would just have to do as much as she could over the next week. It was all the time she could get off from work. She had already run through all her vacation days and paid holidays and the personal days on top of it, trying to take care of her mother toward the end. Right now Julia's boss was still feeling charitable. That wouldn't last forever.

Over the next seven days Julia would gather what

she wanted from this cabin. Then she'd lock the door and leave the rest of it to nature.

And there were her mother's ashes to spread. Annika hadn't specified exactly where, just up at the cabin, *Someplace nice. I know you'll do it right.*

She had asked Julia to do a few other things, too. A short but weighty list of last wishes to fulfill.

Julia would try to do some of them. At least the ones that she believed in.

Flicka moaned and tilted her head back, the way she did whenever Julia found the right spot behind her ears to scratch. But Julia's hand was resting idly on the dog's back at the moment. She had stopped petting her a while ago.

As if to reclaim her territory, Julia scratched behind Flicka's right ear. The dog moaned again. But an icy swish of discomfort still lingered just beneath the surface of Julia's skin.

It was stupid. It wasn't real. This place was already getting to her again.

Julia jumped off the couch and got to work.

It wouldn't do to think too much.

2

The harvest was more than Julia could eat in a month, but she kept plucking and piling more and more into the flat-bottomed basket. Everything looked delicious.

Tomatoes twice the size of anything she could buy in a store. Swiss chard in gorgeous bright colors of green and yellow and red. Heads of broccoli so heavy Julia thought she might have to chop them apart with the ax from the woodpile before she could easily carry them inside.

There were wild onions and a long row of chubby garlic that felt so satisfying to dig up from the dirt. But still the sun was lowering, and Julia had to come to her senses.

She carried the basket from the bottom, using both hands. Her haul was too heavy to trust the handle.

With the last half hour of yellow sunlight, she piled up and carried three armfuls of the slim pieces of wood that would keep the Franklin stove cheerfully blazing throughout the night. Then, just as her mother taught her, she chopped at least enough more to get her through the morning.

Chopping wood and carrying up buckets of water from the stream were as constant a part of Julia's childhood as checking email and refreshing her social media feed were now in her adult life.

She had just that one more chore to do.

As the sun teetered just above the peak, almost ready to slip behind it, Julia grabbed the wooden bucket from the floor just inside the cabin door and hurried with it down to the stream. She knelt on the bank and submerged the bucket in the same deep hole she always used. Then she started carrying the full bucket back up the hill.

Her muscles weren't used to this particular strain on them anymore. She had to set the bucket down several times to stretch out her aching arms. By the time she returned to the cabin, enough water had slopped out of the top that there was only about half a bucket left.

Soft, she could imagine her mother teasing her. City life had made her soft.

Her mother had been hardy almost to the end. Julia had always assumed she would live out here stubbornly alone in the woods until she was at least 90.

She only made it to 53.

The injustice of it could still make Julia's eyes burn.

"Ready for dinner?" she asked the dog. Flicka danced around in a circle with her tail wagging hard. Julia cut open the top of the dog food bag and scooped out a cup of kibble into a wooden bowl.

Maybe there was a specific set of dog bowls somewhere around, but Julia had never lived here with dogs. Her mother got her first one after Julia left, probably because she was lonely.

Julia could see the sense in it. Even hiking here today, it felt good to have Flicka's company. The dog thought everything was exciting. Watching her chase butterflies and grasshoppers and scurry after ground squirrels racing to their burrows, Julia could forget for minutes at a time where she was and why.

After a dinner of bread topped with cheese and slices of bright red tomato, sprinkled lightly with salt and pepper, the way her mother used to make it, Julia fed a few more sticks into the stove and thought about where to sleep.

Her childhood bed looked so small. But the idea of sleeping in her mother's felt strangely intrusive. Flicka settled the matter by launching herself onto Annika's bed and stretching herself the full length of the left side.

Next to the right side of the bed was a small table with a thick white half-melted candle on top of a plate. A box of matches rested beside it, ready for Julia's mother to light it again.

There was a book there, too, with a twig from some tree serving as a bookmark.

One of her mother's old, well-worn guides to herbal remedies.

A lot of good it had done her.

Julia carried the book out to the front room, thinking she would put it back on one of her mother's shelves.

But some impulse made her open the door to the Franklin stove and add it to the rest of the fuel.

Her mother was who she was. There was no changing it, especially not any more.

Julia returned to the larger bedroom and curled up next to her mother's dog.

3

The morning dawned hazy. Julia wasn't entirely surprised. Even though yesterday's sky had been a bright and cloudless blue, she saw on the weather reports she checked before leaving that there were fires burning in New Mexico and southern Colorado.

A shift in the wind, and the smoke had shown up here. Rather than gray or brown, the way she was used to seeing in Denver, here it was a milky-white so thick it completely hid the surrounding peaks.

When Julia was growing up, there were fires only occasionally, spaced out across several years. Now it seemed like the West was always burning, somewhere. This summer alone, there had been massive fires all at the same time in California, Arizona, New Mexico, and Colorado. She pitied the poor fire crews who had to try to be everywhere at once.

Julia's work sometimes touched on that, although she knew better than to think she was actually part of the solution. She worked for an environmental consulting firm that helped developers of planned communities.

Plant trees here. Don't plant them there. Searching for that balance between providing green spaces and not adding more burnable fuel if a fire should suddenly sweep through the suburbs.

At least the air didn't smell smoky. When Julia emerged from the cabin, everything still smelled as fresh and clear as the day before.

But maybe she wouldn't stay the whole week. Not if it was going to be like this. She couldn't remember any rain in the forecast, so there might be nothing to wash the smoke away.

She should front-end her activities. Do what she came here to do. Start going through the cabin, room by room, and packing up what she thought she might like to have.

Probably none of her mother's books, but maybe a few sentimental items of clothing. Julia wouldn't mind having the table her father had made, but getting it down off the mountain might prove too complicated.

But first were the morning chores. Chopping wood, hauling water.

Her forearms and shoulders still ached from doing both yesterday, but pride made her want to improve her methods today—

The wood pile ... was different.

In her haste to finish up, she remembered leaving it more scattered and disorganized than this.

But the sticks she had chopped last night were now neatly stacked in three even rows.

Julia could feel it again, the icy swish through her veins. She blinked and looked at the wood pile through what she hoped were clearer eyes.

Some childish part of her wanted to kick through the neatly-stacked piles and scatter them like before. But what would that prove? Instead she took a deep and steadying breath.

Flicka stood at her side, staring at the same neat stacks with her ears up, panting happily and wagging her tail.

"Oh, don't you start," Julia muttered. She turned around and headed back to the cabin for her bucket.

After a breakfast of bread toasted on top of the stove and some of her mother's raspberry jam, Julia began in the small bedroom, curious what she would find.

Beneath the single window was the small bookcase Julia and her mother had built together. It spanned half the length of the wall, and rose two shelves high.

Here were her *Little House on the Prairie* books. And *Anne of Green Gables. Pippi Longstocking.* God, it was all so quaint.

But also some *Nancy Drews* and *Hardy Boys.* At least those were slightly more modern.

Black Beauty and *Lassie Come Home. The Yearling,* although that book was so thick, she started it but never finished.

There were other books featuring spunky girls with their horses and dogs. Lots of books with old-fashioned covers showing girls wearing pinafores and frocks.

Looking at them all now, Julia could see that she must have grown up bizarrely sheltered.

She remembered being this girl, and yet at the same time it was like unearthing a time capsule someone else buried.

What was her mother thinking? That they really could live here away from the world? That she could keep her daughter from ever knowing how ugly it might be out there away from the mountains and the trees?

Maybe it might have worked if her father hadn't shown up at the cabin one day.

It was the same summer Julia helped her mother build the shower. She was eight then, aware that she had a father somewhere, but not in the least bit curious who he was.

One afternoon a brown-skin man came walking across their meadow. He bore a backpack, and Julia assumed he was just some hiker.

She and her mother were chopping wood at the time, no surprise.

"Would you like some help?" the man asked.

"Hello, Gerardo," Annika answered, wiping the

sweat from her forehead. She added without ceremony, "Julia, this is your father."

Suddenly Julia understood her brown eyes and brown hair. Annika had never described what Gerardo looked like, and for some reason Julia had always been too shy to ask.

Until that visit, Julia sometimes suspected that her mother gave her *Anne of Green Gables* because Julia herself was adopted. There seemed no other explanation for why she didn't have Annika's blonde hair and blue eyes.

"What brings you here?" Annika asked Gerardo.

"An apology," he said. Then looking at Julia he added, "To you."

He stayed exactly one night and slept on the denim couch. Annika was cordial to him, but not overly friendly. Julia took her cue from her mother and mostly listened, but didn't talk.

After a dinner of ratatouille made from a variety of vegetables from Annika's garden, the three of them sat at the fir plank table Gerardo made and he told them a simple story.

He had remarried—a wonderful woman named Ellen—and she had just had a baby a few months before. A little boy named Mateo.

"It made me realize," Gerardo said. But he never finished the sentence. He opened his palms on top of the table and looked at Julia with eyes that seemed sad with regret.

He talked with a slight accent. It sounded musical to Julia's ears. She decided she liked this man. He seemed gentle and kind. She wouldn't mind if he came and visited again.

When he was ready to leave the next morning, Julia and her mother escorted him out to the meadow.

Gerardo looked around them as if admiring the landscape where he used to live.

He asked Annika, "Do you still see them?"

Julia saw her mother's spine stiffen before she answered, "Of course."

Gerardo Rosales said nothing, but he nodded and cast a glance over at Julia.

"She should probably go to school," he said.

"I can teach her fine myself," Annika said.

"Still … I think she should go to school," Gerardo persisted. "And Ellen wants to meet her." Gerardo spoke directly to Julia. "Would you like to come visit us for Christmas?"

And with that, the spell was broken. The outside world came sneaking in.

Annika must have known she couldn't stop it. Her child's father had his rights.

Julia met her half-brother and her step-mother that Christmas. And she started visiting them every year.

First for a week, then several, and by the time she was twelve, it was the whole month of December.

Ellen was lovely. Smart and cool and fun. And Julia enjoyed being a big sister to first Mateo and then Sophia a few years later.

Compromises were made. The spring and summer were for Annika and Julia, alone up on the mountain. But fall and winter, Annika rented a small house in town and worked as a server while Julia attended school.

But just those few months of socializing and civilization weren't enough for Julia anymore. When she was 14, she announced that she wanted to live with her father.

"I'll still visit you in the winter," Julia said. "But only if you live in town."

She had no interest in returning to the primitive conditions of living in a cabin with no running water or electricity.

Julia understood now how it must have broken her mother's heart.

But Annika had her *friends*, didn't she? Her special work. Her special gift.

Julia had always been outside of all of that. Maybe a bitter part of her had been glad she could make her mother miss her.

She was just a child. Fourteen. Julia hoped the last year had made up for all of it.

She rose from where she'd been sitting on the floor and left her old books where they were. If she wanted to reread them, she could buy them again. There was nothing unique about these copies. She had to limit how much she brought back.

She wandered out to the main room and took a look at her mother's bookshelves after all. Flicka was stretched out on the couch, napping. It was almost lunchtime. After some food and another cup of black coffee, Julia would take herself and the dog out for a walk.

But first she should finish the rest of this chore. Then she could check it off her list.

There were more books here than she remembered. It made sense. Her mother had always been a reader. Maybe she would have brought even more books back from her supply runs to town once Julia left to live with her father.

There were nature books, books on plants and herbs, and a whole section devoted to philosophers. Julia's eyes scanned the titles. There was nothing she particularly hungered to read.

Annika's own books, twelve of them published over the last ten years, sat lined up in a row. *Notes from the Outpost Away from the World,* Volumes 1, 2, 3 …

Julia already had copies of all of those. She had read each of them numerous times.

And here, next to them, were the five books Julia

remembered so vividly from her childhood. *The Story of Findhorn. Findhorn Revealed. The Mystics of Findhorn.* Et cetera, et cetera.

"It's a magical place," her mother told her, showing her the beautiful pictures of the Findhorn garden. "It's a Garden of Eden," Annika said, then explained what the Garden of Eden was.

Julia had heard and read the story so many times, she could recite it now from memory. In 1962, a man named Peter Caddy moved with his wife Eileen and their friend Dorothy Maclean to a rugged, sandy, desolate caravan park on the shore of Findhorn Bay in northern Scotland.

They were drawn there by some mystical force to conduct a great experiment.

Both Eileen Caddy and Dorothy Maclean were clairvoyants. *Clear seers.* Each had been given a vision of the garden they could create on that barren ground.

Within the first year, they were growing such a great abundance of fruits and vegetables, people started coming from all over the world to gawk at what they had done.

When asked how they did it, Peter Caddy was cagey at first. "Special blend of compost," he told some of them. "Just good luck," he told others.

And then finally one day he began telling the "truth."

His mystical wife and their friend were communicating with the nature spirits.

They could see them, Eileen and Dorothy (who started calling themselves Elixir and Divina). They spoke to the sprites and the elves and the devas. They could see the little creatures encouraging all the plants to grow.

Other mystics came then, too, and they confirmed that the creatures were real.

Many of them wrote books, describing the different classifications of nature spirits, from the devas on down to the little wood sprites who lived under logs.

Of course many people thought the Caddys and Maclean were crazy. They dismissed the claims out of hand.

But others bought it completely. A spiritual community began to grow in Findhorn, with disciples as abundant as the garden's plants.

"I see them, too," Annika had told Julia from the time Julia was small. "And since you're my daughter, I'm sure you'll be able to see them if you try."

Julia did try. Every day, hour upon hour, year after year.

"There's one!" Annika would cry, pointing off toward some tree. "See her? She's about two feet tall, dressed all in green."

Annika drew pictures to try to help Julia. She

created a classification book just for her. Julia studied it all the time, hoping one day her eyesight would clear and she'd see one for herself.

Starting with the Brownies, who liked to come into the cabin to watch how the humans lived.

"They look like little men," Annika said. "About a foot tall. They usually wear little brown jackets, brown pants, and brown boots. They watch us do housework, and then they copy us while we're asleep."

It was the Brownies who tidied up at night, picking up clothes from the floor, sweeping up crumbs.

If Annika were here now, she would say the Brownies had stacked Julia's wood overnight.

They were also known to love communing with animals, especially cats and dogs.

It was a Brownie, Annika would have said, who scratched Flicka behind the ears yesterday afternoon while they sat on the couch.

Brownies who kept this cabin so clean, even though it should have looked dusty and abandoned after sitting unused for over a year.

It was all crazy. Utterly crazy.

Julia turned from the bookcase. She had seen enough.

"Come on, girl," she called to Flicka, then she stalked out of the cabin.

The dog trotted happily at her side as Julia walked off some of her anger.

They passed her mother's garden. A garden as lush and prolific as the one at Findhorn, made, Annika claimed, the same way.

"Do you see her?" Annika would ask, pointing. "That little tomato sprite hugging the vine?"

"No," Julia had to admit time and time again. She never saw any of them. Not even once.

But with maturity, and exposure to the real life away from their isolated cabin, Julia gradually came to understand what Gerardo Rosales had realized, too.

Annika Ross was a kook. Maybe not clinically crazy, but not fully sane.

Maybe she had a more vivid imagination than anyone else. Or maybe she was more suggestible. One day she read a book about Findhorn and convinced herself it was real.

Was she a clairvoyant, like she claimed? Julia doubted that, too. Her mother saw what she wanted to see, and that was all it was.

None of it would have mattered if Annika hadn't gotten sick. She could have lived her life wrapped in fantasy until she was 90, as far as Julia was concerned.

But the truth was, Julia loved her mother. And when she learned of the diagnosis, she flew to Annika's side. And for months last year Julia begged her to put away her nonsense and let the doctors help.

No to chemo. No to radiation. No to surgery, even though it might have bought her more time.

It was glioblastoma, an aggressive form of brain cancer. It killed Annika just fourteen months after she learned she had it.

She said no to any kind of treatment, but said yes to moving in with Julia in her apartment in Denver so the two of them could be together.

The decline was brutal to watch. Julia never wanted to think of it again. But by the end of Annika's life, both of them seemed to have said all they needed to say.

I love you.

I love you, too, Mom. So much.

Over and over again.

Now her mother was reduced to ashes inside a bag, waiting in Julia's backpack for her to find the right place to spread them.

Julia slowed her walk. The anger was gone. But she still headed for the woods.

If it was here, the right place to leave her mother behind, she hoped she would feel it, hoped she would know.

Here where her mother had tried to show her so many times where the elves and sprites and devas were frolicking among the trees.

5

Later, when Julia and Flicka emerged from her fruitless search in the woods, the milky-white haze was gone, replaced by a thin gray film that covered the blue sky.

Julia could see the peaks again, although she thought she could smell the first tinge of smoke in the air.

It reminded her to keep working. To get her job done, in case things got worse and she wanted to leave sooner.

She returned to the cabin and her mother's books. Maybe she should take these twelve volumes of Annika's own work, even if Julia could buy as many more copies as she wanted. She flipped through the first two, imagining Annika holding her newly-published books in her hands.

It had been the idea of the herbalist in Altar Peak who had published a few books of her own. She showed Annika how to format the manuscript, how to upload her drawings and photographs and make her own cover, and one day out of the blue Julia got a package in the mail with her mother's first paperback book.

It was much like the Findhorn books, full of daily notes about the garden and lots of side information about the various nature spirits Julia had heard about all her life.

At first Julia was embarrassed. She didn't want her mother to expose herself this way. And Julia certainly didn't want anyone she knew to find out what her mother was like.

But over time, as the volumes continued coming, Julia began to read them with a detached sort of curiosity. A window into her mother's mind.

Her mother wrote about Julia sometimes. Nothing negative, just sweet and folksy stories. Annika never told her readers—and that number was growing year by year—that her daughter had left her and not come back.

Annika Ross's popularity with a certain crowd seemed to take her by surprise. Her herbalist friend had warned her that might happen.

"Never tell them exactly where you live," the woman said. "I've had people show up at my shop that I wished had never heard of me."

So Annika was careful to describe the location of the cabin in only the most general terms.

But it wasn't enough. That was why there was now a lock on the cabin door.

Some fan had followed the clues and made himself at home over the winter. When Annika returned from her season in town, she found him settled in and waiting for her.

It was only the strenuous objection of her very large, very protective dog Brute that convinced the man he should leave.

After Brute came Flicka. Julia couldn't imagine the sweet Lab chasing anyone off. More likely Flicka would sidle up to them, hoping to have her ears scratched.

Julia finished stacking her mother's books on the floor of the smaller bedroom. They were too heavy to carry out in her backpack, but she already planned on using the wooden-sided wagon her mother kept for her supply runs into town.

It was well past noon, and her belly and head were complaining. A cup of coffee, another tomato sandwich, and she'd be ready to work the rest of the afternoon.

Leaving time, of course, for chopping wood and

hauling water. Always, always, never a day off.

While she stood at the thick wooden counter in the tiny kitchen slicing two more hefty red tomatoes, she heard Flicka moan behind her. Julia whipped around to find out why.

The dog was doing it again, groaning in contentment with her head tipped back and her eyes closed.

As if some little man dressed in all brown clothes were scratching her vigorously behind her left ear.

Julia pointed her knife at the space just above the dog. "Stop that. I can see you. Stop that."

She didn't know why she did it.

Maybe she was light-headed from hunger or caffeine-deprived without her second cup of coffee.

Maybe this place was getting to her. Making her a little crazy.

But the dog opened her eyes and looked at Julia before settling her chin back on one of the red cushions to resume her snooze.

There was no more groaning. No more head tipped back in ecstasy.

Julia resumed her slicing.

Sandwich and coffee made, she sat at the fir plank table to eat her lunch. All through the meal, she stared at the sleeping dog.

Dammit, she hated herself for this. But no one was around. No one would know.

She broke off part of her crust and tore it into little pieces. Then she scattered them on top of the table.

She tipped her mug of coffee, spilling some of it on the wood.

"Come on, Flicka," she said, standing up briskly and striding toward the door.

She would chop her wood now and get it out of the way. And give the imaginary Brownie a chance to work.

6

———

Julia's arms and back ached as she brought down the ax time and again. But she had to admit to feeling satisfied by the effort. All this sweat came from doing something useful, not just working out in a gym. No wonder her mother always seemed so strong. It was because, in fact, she was.

Even after only a day, Julia's appetite was adjusting to her outdoor life. After stacking the wood to bring inside later, she headed for her mother's garden to find something to eat.

Normally by mid-afternoon, Julia might have a bag of M&M's to get her through the rest of the day. Her job involved brain work, not physical labor. She sat at her desk for hours doing research and writing reports.

It had been part of her rebellion to decide to get her

degree in botany. A way of separating herself from the crazy ideas her mother had.

Science was real. The laws of nature were knowable. Plants grew because of sunlight and water, not because garden elves loved them.

Julia spotted the furry tops of carrots and pulled up three. They were the purple kind her mother liked to grow. Julia brushed off the dirt and ate them in less than a minute while she searched for more to eat.

She was craving a salad of all of these greens. The chard and broccoli she had already harvested and the beans she now spotted growing in the corner. She plucked at least a dozen and cradled them in the hem of her shirt.

The first time she ate food out in the real world, she had a stomach ache for days. Her body could barely process it—especially the meat.

When she returned to the mountain and confessed to her mother, Annika said it was because normally she was eating light.

Light as in illumination, not as in fat-free and slimming. Julia had accepted the answer at the time.

Now she wondered about it again. Whether there was something to what her mother said. Maybe calling all the feast of the garden eating light was too woo-woo, but eating only plants for so many years must have done both her mother and Julia some good.

The brain cancer was just a bitch. That was the only

way Julia could explain it. Her mother hadn't done anything "wrong," but still the cancer had claimed her.

It was like forest fires, in a way. Sometimes they were manmade, from people carelessly leaving campfires burning or throwing a cigarette butt into the woods.

But sometimes they were caused by lightning, especially dry lighting without any rain. Mother Nature could be a bitch, too. Although Julia never shared that theory with any of her professors.

At one time she had thought about going into academia herself. She went on from her bachelors to get her masters, but stopped before going all the way to a Ph.D.

Somewhere along the way she had lost the desire. Or maybe she realized she had already proved her point. She knew a lot about the same subjects her mother pursued in a completely opposite way.

Maybe at some point their paths crossed in the middle. For whatever reason, by the time Annika died, Julia no longer needed to prove anything to her mother.

7

—————

Wood chopped, belly filled, water hauled—it was time for Julia to return to the cabin.

Once again she opened the door and stood on the threshold, nervous about going inside.

She crossed to the table. And swore.

It wasn't possible. All of this was made up.

The crumbs were gone. The spilled coffee had been wiped away.

Julia swore again, loudly and colorfully to the room. It felt good to let it out.

She sank onto the couch next to Flicka, who had resumed her position the moment she entered the house.

A flicker of fear shocked Julia's nervous system.

This wasn't cute. What if it was real?

If not for how she was raised, Julia might have thought it was the ghost of her mother, come back to clean her own roost.

But how was that any saner of an explanation?

It was all just a matter of your beliefs.

Pick a reason: God, angels, ghosts, spirits—Brownies—why should any of them sound more believable than the others?

Clairvoyant. *Clear seeing.*

My God, was Julia finally starting to see for herself?

Not the little men and girlish green sprites flitting around the woods and melting into the trees.

But the *effects* of them. The observable effects of those invisible creatures.

It wasn't possible, yet maybe it was.

Julia leaned forward on the couch and rested her forehead on her hands.

She had been here just twenty-four hours, and already she was losing her mind.

But the *crumbs.* And the coffee spill.

That table hadn't cleaned itself.

8

When she gathered up the wood for the night, Julia deliberately left the rest of the pile in disarray.

"Show me," she said out loud, but softly. Flicka wagged her tail as if Julia had been talking to her.

For dinner, Julia made the huge salad she had been craving for the past few hours. She ate it without dressing, just raw and delicious. She could almost feel the light coursing through her bloodstream again.

She rearranged the pile of her mother's books on the floor of her old bedroom, pushing every third book off at an angle. Let some little Brownie look at it and decide it all needed to be straightened again.

This must be how parents felt, having fun hiding

Easter eggs all over their house. Julia deliberately looked for things she could put askew to see if anyone cared to make them right.

"I'm losing it," she told the dog as they both settled into bed. Flicka stretched out on her side of the bed and put her head on the extra pillow. Julia slung her arm over the dog and slept hard.

In the morning—

In the morning. Julia cruised from room to room while she waited for her coffee to brew and counted all the Easter eggs that had been found.

Every single thing that had been out of place was now tidied and set to right.

"Good job," she said to the air.

And felt slightly less foolish than yesterday when she told the invisible beings at the woodpile, "Show me."

Coffee mug in hand, she went out to inspect the work there. Just like the morning before, all the wood was neatly stacked in three separate rows.

"Are there three of you?" she asked out loud. "Or just one of you, but you like the way it looks?"

She saw nothing, she heard nothing—but the evidence was there. That wood hadn't stacked itself.

Why hadn't she done it this way as a child?

But Julia immediately knew the answer.

She didn't have to back then—she *believed.* She

thought the only reason she couldn't see them was because of her.

It still felt unsettling. Scary. She wasn't wholeheartedly ready to throw herself into this boat.

And there was still the other theory to consider: that this was somehow her mother's spirit doing the chores.

"Mom, if it's you," Julia said as she walked back toward the cabin, "you're going to have to show me. I'm pretty lost here."

Flicka gave a short bark and pounced on a bright green grasshopper.

"Was that it?" Julia asked. "Was that some kind of sign?"

She waited a moment, watching the dog watch the grasshopper bounce away.

Julia ran a hand over her eyes. Her head was starting to hurt.

For the first time that morning she looked up at the sky.

The milky-white haze was back, even thicker than yesterday's. And the air smelled of smoke.

But she wasn't ready to leave. Things were starting to get interesting. Julia wanted to stay the remaining five days.

But the mountain peaks were missing. The sky was missing. This haze of milky white smoke above her wasn't normal.

"Do you see this?" she asked her unseen friends. "Should I be worried? Are any of you worried?"

Julia returned to her cabin, uneasy with all the silence.

9

Spread the ashes.

Pack up what I want.

Tell the woods and the garden what happened to my mother.

There were a few more items on Julia's to-do list, but until now, that third one hadn't made the cut.

Her mother had asked her to do it. "They won't understand," she said. "They'll think I just walked off and abandoned them."

"Well … didn't you say goodbye when you left last year?" Julia asked, humoring her dying mother.

"'Goodbye and I'll see you soon,'" Annika answered. "The same thing I tell them when I move into town in the winter."

Even after Julia went to college and stopped visiting

198

her mother over the winter, Annika had gotten used to spending a few months in town. She had a few friends and there were her books to type up and publish.

That was Julia's task for today: to find her mother's handwritten notebooks that later became the books.

Annika would sit at the kitchen table every night and record everything she saw and did during the day.

But no matter where she searched, Julia couldn't find the spiral notebooks. Maybe they were in town somewhere, although Annika didn't always rent the same house.

Or maybe she had burned them, although that seemed unlikely. Annika always liked keeping her records.

"Attention," Julia said as she stood in the middle of the main room. "My mother's notebooks are missing. Do you know where they are?"

And then it occurred to her the Brownies might not understand English.

Or really, human speech of any kind. Why should she assume that they did? It was the same egotistical thinking that made people believe that aliens visiting from another universe would understand our language.

So Julia brought out one of her own notebooks that she carried inside her backpack.

She pointed to it. "This. Find them? Help me?"

Julia chuckled to herself. What a fool.

But who was going to laugh at her? Flicka didn't speak human, either.

As if in answer, the black Lab moaned. Someone or something was scratching her behind the ear.

"Go ahead," she told the Brownie. "Don't let me stop you. But—" she pointed to the notebook again. "Can you help me?"

Flicka sighed and dropped her head back onto the pillow.

Julia was getting nowhere. But at least she was getting there faster than the day before.

"Listen, I need to tell you something," she surprised herself by saying. Was she really going to just blurt it out? Right here and now?

If the Brownie didn't understand English or human speech, it really didn't matter what she said.

"My mother ... Annika Ross ... you know her ..."

Julia cleared her throat. She wanted to do this right.

"She's ... she got sick. Last year. And she really thought she was coming back. But ... I'm sorry, but she died last month. I'm her daughter Julia. Maybe you remember me."

Julia cleared her throat again. She was still standing in the middle of the room, like she was there to give a speech.

"She ... really loved you. She told me that all the time. She asked me to come back here and tell you that. And to tell you she said goodbye."

Julia stopped talking. She stood as still as she could and held her breath and tried to listen.

What did she expect to hear? Some little sob from over by the couch?

She heard nothing. She saw nothing. Still.

"Okay, so … I just needed to tell you that. I'm sorry. I … really miss her, too."

Julia's voice caught. She cleared her throat again. "Yeah, so … okay. I guess that's all."

She left her notebook on the table and wandered out the door. She didn't feel right remaining inside while the Brownie might be silently grieving.

I'm crazy. This is crazy. I'm losing it.

But at the moment, Julia felt better than she had in weeks.

The air outside the cabin felt heavy. The milky white had turned a dirtier shade of gray. A light breeze was blowing, but it hadn't cleared the thick film from the sky.

Julia still couldn't see any of the mountains. It was unnerving to find the familiar landscape so completely erased.

She could smell the smoke now, there was no mistaking it.

My God, was there a fire somewhere closer than she expected?

She had no way of checking. No computer, no cell phone, no contact whatsoever with the outside world.

Maybe she should leave. Go right now. Pack up her pack and the wagon and go.

Julia looked around her. Searching for answers. For some kind of advice.

She hadn't sprinkled her mother's ashes yet. She had to do that.

If this place burned—

If there was nothing to come back to—

She had to do at least that much.

Julia rushed back into the cabin. She dug out the bag of ashes from inside her pack.

On the table her notebook was open. She was sure she had left it closed.

A blank page had been ripped down the center, leaving just the bottom inch of it still intact.

Some kind of message? *I'm torn, I'm ripped? You have torn my Brownie heart in two?*

"Is there a fire coming?" Julia asked the unseen ripper. "Can you or the others see it? I have to know!"

Flicka slapped her tail nervously against the couch. She must have heard something in Julia's voice.

"I don't want to leave!" Julia said to the room. "But I have to if it isn't safe."

The door to the Franklin stove sprang open.

Flames sputtered and licked at the metal.

That was a sign. That meant something. That wasn't normal. That didn't just happen.

"Okay," Julia said, her breath coming out too hard.

She could feel her heart racing. "Okay, I think you just told me yes."

Fire was coming. "How long do I have?" she asked her invisible guide.

The door to the Franklin stove banged once. Twice. Three times.

"Three … hours? Three days?"

But it couldn't be three days. The sky was a blanket of smoke. Julia could see it and smell it for herself.

"Three hours," she said, and the stove door banged shut all the way.

"Right," Julia said. "Oh my God."

10

The wagon would be too heavy to pull. It would slow her down. She needed speed.

She quickly paged through the stack of her mother's books, to check for any handwritten notes, anything personal.

Mother Nature was a *bitch*. Why did the fire have to come here now? Just as Julia was finally making some headway? What she wouldn't have given for these kinds of experiences when she was a child. Some way of knowing that her mother wasn't crazy.

Even more, proof that Julia could see it for herself, too. If not the little creatures, than at least evidence of what they could do.

All that wasted time. All those terrible feelings. The separation from her mother. Everything was so wrong.

There was no time to spread the ashes. She would have to bring those with her.

No time to tell the woods or the garden that her mother was dead.

And then somehow one hour was already two. Julia was too scattered. She was running around the cabin picking up this and that, afraid to let any of it go, but she had to go.

The dog watched her nervously, sometimes panting, usually wagging her tail. As though she were in trouble for any and all of this. Julia paused to give Flicka a reassuring pat.

"We're leaving in a minute. It'll be okay. I just need to—" Julia swallowed a sob. "It's just hard to leave. This was my home. This was my mother's." But she wiped her sweating eyes and steeled herself at last.

She picked up the pack. It held as little and as much as she could reasonably take. Then she called for the dog. "Flicka come. We have to hurry."

Somehow the sky had closed in while Julia busied herself in the cabin. A dark brown dome blotted out the mountains.

The wind was blowing harder now. Julia could smell the smoke coming up from the south.

She could also see, in place of the hidden mountains, a glow of orange behind the dome of brown smoke.

She had six miles to hike. Four miles south before the trail turned slightly west.

Four miles in the direction of the hot orange glow.

Julia crouched on the ground. Her heart was pounding too hard for her to stand at the moment.

Her mother had taught her about this. What to do if they were ever caught in a fire.

Run to the stream. Immerse yourself. Wet your clothes, your body, your hair.

And then?

It depended.

Run if it looked like you had time.

Stay put in the water if it looked like you didn't.

Flicka whined and licked Julia's cheek. The poor dog's heart might be pounding, too. Julia was supposed to take care of both of them. Her mother had left this dog and this cabin in Julia's hands.

Six miles was too far. They weren't going to make it.

"Come on!" Julia shouted as she started running for the stream.

The Franklin stove had said she had three hours.

But what did the stove—or the Brownie—really know?

Mother Nature was a bitch. She had all the control here.

Julia ran with her pack and the dog to the water.

The stream was shallow in long stretches, but there

were places where the bottom was deep enough to sink down to.

Julia led the dog along the bank, searching for one of those spots. Already the smoke was heavy enough it burned her eyes and made it harder to see.

"Here!" Julia slid off the bank into the water. She held out her arms to encourage Flicka to follow.

The dog backed away, nervous again. Julia made kissing noises. The dog still resisted.

"Flicka!" Julia cried. "Come on!" Then she reached up and grabbed the Lab by the collar.

Flicka fought her, but Julia persisted. The dog might hate her, but at least she might live.

As soon as the dog reached the water, Julia started dunking her and splashing her to get all her fur covered.

She could hear it now, as the flames came roaring up the mountain. Like someone opening a furnace as big as a stadium.

The smoke burned her eyes, it burned her lungs. She dove beneath the water and pulled the dog with her.

When she came up for air, she could see the flames eating through the woods. Her mother's woods, black and orange on top of the green.

But she saw something else. She could see the cabin in the distance.

And a light surrounding it, like a dome.

It was bright green, with streaks of yellow and white.

It covered the entire cabin and the garden beyond.

Like a giant green cup someone had inverted over the structure, keeping the smoke and the flames away.

Julia's lungs and eyes burned. She dunked herself and the dog again.

When she came up she could see the flames trying to get in. But the bright green dome repulsed them. The fire could not get through.

The flames surrounded the dome, hungry for the wood and the fuel inside.

But then the fire started to sputter and spit. As if something were wetting it from underneath.

Julia bobbed in and out of the water for the next half hour, watching the cabin and the garden fight off the flames.

Julia waited another hour before daring to leave the stream.

The dog hopped out and shook herself several times before looking up at Julia and wagging her tail.

The ground was still hot. Julia could feel it coming through the soles of her boots. But she couldn't wait any longer. She had to see.

The green dome was gone. The cabin stood upright and whole. A circle of charred grass extended all around it.

Some of the plants in the garden looked wilted

from the heat, but the flames hadn't touched them at all.

Julia sank to her knees on the cold clean wood of the cabin porch. She gazed all around her at the devastation.

The dome had been real. She saw it with her own eyes.

This cabin was real. And the garden. And this beautiful, sweet-faced dog.

Was it her mother who did this? Was it elves? Brownies? Sprites?

Julia covered her eyes and let herself cry.

11

The list wasn't that long.

Solar panels.

Seeds.

A warmer coat.

A place to rent in the winter.

Dog food.

A new set of sheets.

Julia continued making her list.

It wasn't possible to go back to the city. Not after what she had seen.

Well, okay, she might go back for just a week, to gather up the things she would need.

Quitting her job had been the easiest part. Her heart had never been in it from the start.

No boyfriend. A lease that was almost up anyway.

Julia had research she needed to do.

Maybe for a Ph.D. one of these days. Maybe for the next book in her mother's series.

Notes from the Outpost Away from the World, by Julia Ross Rosales, volume 13.

The woods would take time to heal. But Julia suspected there might be some help to bring the trees back.

She wanted to be there to watch and record it all.

To see with her own eyes what was true.

When she opened her pack after the fire, she found her mother's ashes soaked inside their bag.

So Julia took them back to the water and spread them there. Her mother was right, she would know it when she saw it.

"To my beautiful, complicated mother," Julia said in the waning light. "Whoever can hear me, she told me to tell you goodbye. She loved all of you—probably as much as she loved me. And she sent me to you, so you could show me who you are."

If any of them answered, Julia didn't hear them. If any of them cried for the loss of Annika Ross, Julia didn't know.

But she slept in her mother's bed that night, in a cabin her friends had saved from the fire.

And in the morning, Julia could see the mountain peaks again.

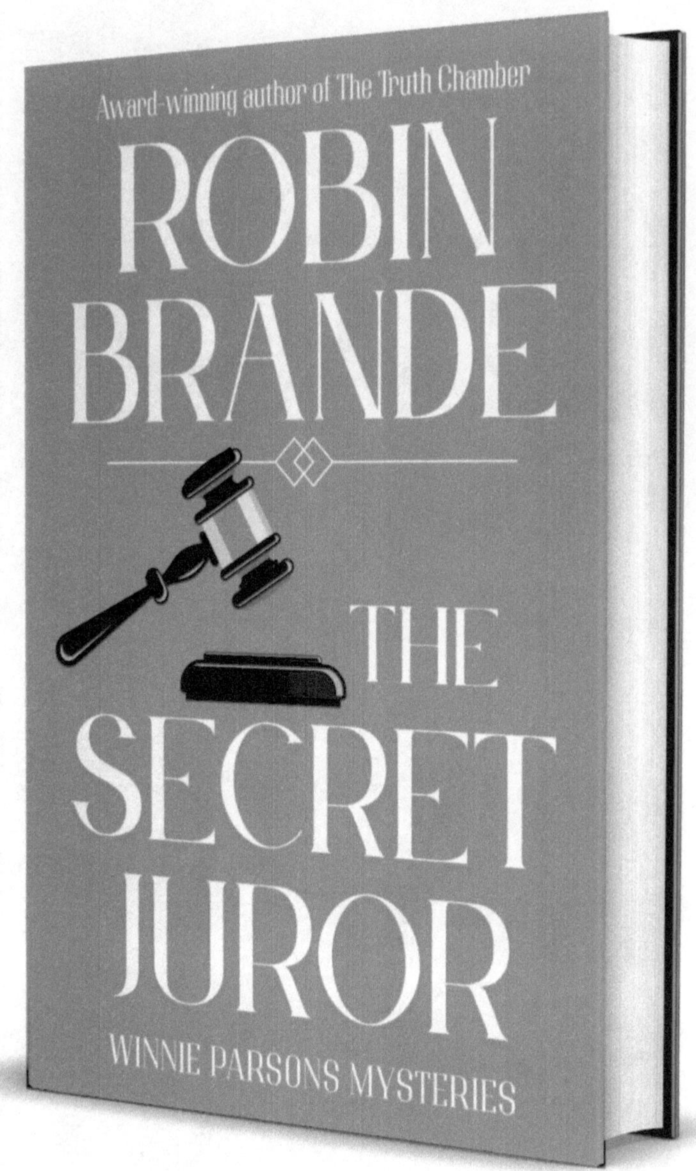

Liars can't hide
from Winnie Parsons.
But they sure keep trying.

The mind is a mysterious place. And the truth can change your life.

Stories of life after death, miracle healings, communication with other species, and more.

Open up your heart
to the love of a
good dog.

ABOUT THE AUTHOR

Robin Brande is an award-winning author, former trial attorney, black belt in martial arts, wilderness medic, and Reiki Master.

She writes in multiple genres, including mystery, fantasy, science fiction, young adult, romance, and self-help. She is also a designer and maker whose work celebrates the bookish life.

For more information:
robinbrande.com